Time in a Bottle

The Resonance

A Novel by:

Raymond Rice

Strategic Book Publishing and Rights Co.

Strategic Book Publishing and Rights Co.
12620 FM 1960, Suite A4-507
Houston, TX 77065
www.sbpra.com

ISBN: 978-1-61204-166-7

Design: Dedicated Book Services, Inc. (www.netdbs.com)

For Mandee, Anja, Mila and Jude.

Thank you for your amazing love, your support and for believing in me.

Thank you Mom, for always encouraging me to dream.

And many thanks to the rest of my family.

.

Part I
DISARRAY

"This is the strangest life I've ever known."
—(Jim Morrison)

CHAPTER 1

The rain came down in icy sheets and covered the crooked mountain road in a few inches of frosted water. The ebony night sky held no moon behind the dense cloud cover. There was only rain and blackness.

An older red pickup truck made its way along the road. The dim headlights winced and struggled through the downpour, their light reflecting off of the many large trees. The truck picked up speed as it crossed the crest of the highest peak and headed downward; downward toward Canyon Lake, some nine to twelve hundred feet below.

Small patches of dirty white slush reflected back from the cliff side of the road, fuzzy in the vehicle's muted light. Water blanketed the windshield, despite the furious slashing of the wipers. The two people had been traveling for a few hours, and the storm had become increasingly wet and intense.

There was a faint flicker to the side of the road as the truck approached a sweeping corner. The quick movement caught the attention of the passenger. "Look out!"

Something darted in front of the truck. It was a fast blur in the heavy rain. The brakes squealed and the back wheels broke free into a hydroplane. The truck slid quickly across the road as the two passengers sped towards the guardrail. There was a loud crash like the snapping of dry brittle bones as the faded red truck smashed through the wood and metal barrier and dove over the side of the tall mountain, its lights shining through the foggy rain and casting a dim glow over the lake as it fell.

CHAPTER 2

There was a bright flash of brilliant white light, like the mid-day summer sun reflecting off of a freshly cleaned mirror. And then it was gone.

CHAPTER 3

A long, thin road slowly wound its way from the top of the plush forested hill to a parking lot at lakeside. The somewhat secluded lake sat beneath the peaks of the large hills that encompassed it like a bowl. The lake itself was thickly lined with trees and deep green plants.

The lake water reflected a pale blue sky and several cotton puff clouds. Although Canyon Lake was a popular spot for recreation in the late summer, at this time it was not crowded with people. Many had already begun preparing for fall, or were not yet back from their out of state homes for the university school year.

A few couples stood and talked. An elderly woman, who was wearing a gold and green sweat suit, power walked the perimeter of the greenbelt with short, quick steps. Her feet barely left the well groomed, blacktopped path. A local man wearing a faded and torn baseball cap fished from shore, casting and slowly reeling. There were no waterskiing families scaring the fish with their noise and large wakes. It was unbelievably peaceful at the lake.

Two teenagers, one with long blond dreadlocks that were pulled back into a ponytail, the other wearing a black T-shirt with a large red skull on it, ducked out of sight behind a redwood tree to smoke a joint. No one paid any particular attention, nor would most of them have really cared.

Kennedy Jones, a man in his early thirties, carried a worn canvas briefcase with a plastic inner liner and enjoyed the light breeze as he strolled around the lake. He hummed softly to himself the last tune he had heard before leaving the house, "Love Me Two Times," by The Doors. He was an educated connoisseur of all types of music, but he always loved to hear the classics from the 1960s and 1970s. He figured that it was a holdover from being born in late 1967, following the 'Summer of Love.' His mother had lived thirty miles or so from Woodstock in Upstate New York, but she moved him to San Francisco in 1974.

Kennedy considered himself to be a Northern Californian at heart, although he had come to accept and enjoy the much smaller town of Eugene, Oregon and all of its little idiosyncrasies. It was not quite as extreme as Berkeley, and maybe at times that was a good thing, but there was still that familiar nonconformist and countercultural attitude present. Eugene was now his home.

He walked toward a tall tree with a wooden park bench in front of it. He noticed people here and there, but none of them really caught his attention. He was preoccupied with thoughts of other things. *Where had the time gone?*

Kennedy sat down, laying his well used briefcase beside him. That same briefcase had carried all of his papers throughout his many years in college. He peered across the lake's surface, watching the muted sunshine ripple past the tiny blue and green peaks.

The lake was nearly still as the last two fishermen pulled their small rowboat up onto the shore near the concrete boat ramp. They reminded Kennedy of a day long since passed, when people might have fished the lake for their main source of food. A time before high speed shopping markets; a time before computers greeted you with pseudo-emotional, pre-recorded messages as if they were your long lost friends. He thought of what it must have been like before everyone became finely tuned, disposable cogs in the tightly wound machine that was the modern world.

Kennedy leaned forward and put his head in his hands, rubbing them lightly across his slightly graying beard, then over his face, and finally through his shoulder length hair. He let out a forceful sigh as he sat up, grabbed his briefcase, and opened it. He pulled some paperwork from it, and then he reached for a pair of black bifocal reading glasses in the pocket of his corduroy sport coat. He began to analyze the papers before him. There were lists of names, times and numbers printed on the pages. A green and gold college logo was printed in the center, at the top of each page. Upon closer inspection, one could see that it was a stylishly made capital letter "O."

"Jesus. I can't believe how many students are enrolled for courses this Fall Term," he said to himself. "How am I supposed to grade all of those papers, even with an assistant?" After a brief pause he said aloud, "And what about the office hours? I'll never be home." He grabbed the bridge of his nose and squinted slightly. He thought again of the fishermen, and then he relaxed. His voice echoed softly in his head. *Don't ignore where you are in search of where you'll be; the future comes soon enough.* He had read that once in a fortune cookie or something, he couldn't quite remember, but the phrase had always stuck with him and it had some meaning for him.

With that thought, he took another slow look at the lake, panning across the small land masses that poked out of the water like turtles about to come up for air. He scanned the large rocks near the center and finally turned to see the parking lot far off in the distance, to the right of the lake from where he was sitting. If he had learned anything in his thirty plus years of existence, it was to enjoy the moment before it had a chance to slip away. What did the classic rock band Grass Roots say, "Live for today?"

Kennedy had agreed to teach several additional courses and seminars over the past few years and they had taken their toll on him. However, that extra work load would pay off soon enough. With Labor Day only a week away, he knew that soon he'd be back in the swing of early September; lecturing, grading papers, and trying to teach the masses of undergraduate students something about literature, written communication and ethics, and hoping that some of them might actually read the material instead of going to the Cliff Notes, Spark Notes or some other form of modern day shortcuts.

Kennedy was up for tenure, and nothing could have made him happier than becoming a permanent fixture at the University of Oregon. He was a Duck, through and through. Kennedy smiled when he thought of his name on the register as a fully credentialed professor. No more adjunct assignments or assistantships. No more late evening or Saturday classes to teach. No more covering for another professor at the last minute so that someone else could enjoy a round of golf on the first sunny day after a long rainy spell.

He had paid his dues and now it was time for his reward. *Dr. Kennedy Jones? Or, does Professor Kennedy Jones sound better?* He let out a small chuckle at the thought. Actually, he'd been called both by students and faculty alike. But there was to be a new meaning to the title, a new found sense of pride, once the professorship became final.

What would he do with that newfound status and money? Write another book? Take a trip somewhere tropical? Add a hot tub to the back deck? Or maybe, just maybe, he'd be lucky enough to fly down to San Francisco for a Giants' National League Championship or even a World Series game. And if they won, well, that would be the perfect icing on the cake. Of course it had been several decades since the Giants had won it, and never since moving to the city of San Francisco in 1958, but it doesn't hurt to dream.

Besides, it wasn't just the faculty and administration that had noticed his dedication. The students had always loved him. They thought of him as a kind, fatherly figure. They'd say, "He's a nice guy," or the "hippy teacher." He's the guy who doesn't eat meat, doesn't wear leather, hangs around the outdoor Town Market every Saturday morning and sips cabernet at his home as he listens to the two hour 'Dead Air' music show on the University station every Saturday evening at seven.

Some of the older students would say that they remembered seeing him in the late 1980s dancing at Autzen Stadium when the Grateful Dead were in town. Some of the other students swore that they saw him doing the same thing at a show at the Shoreline Amphitheater in the San Francisco Bay Area. Of course, being a teacher with summers off can make for fun travels. And, even though the long hours of the University job had started to wear on him, he couldn't have chosen a more entertaining and rewarding life.

The tall trees around the lake emitted a light scent as the breeze picked up suddenly and rushed past him. Cedar. That smell always reminded him of Big Basin Redwood Park, outside of Santa Cruz, California, and it made him feel warm inside. He was lost for a brief moment in a day long since gone by of walking along the Santa Cruz Beach Boardwalk, the morning sun warm on his face and his naked chest, the fog just finishing burning off, and a light ocean breeze caressing his skin. There were families lined up to ride the "Big Dipper" or the "Wild Mouse" and later in the day, when it had gotten warm, the "Log Ride."

Something caught his attention just above the lake and pulled him back from his daydream. A large white bird, somewhat resembling a heron, slowly and gracefully landed in the water on the edge of a small island near the middle of the lake. It leaned down to peck for insects. Its reflection shined back in the water along with the faint red and gold tones of sunset. Kennedy was taken back by the bird's beauty and agility. It had the fluid movements of a much smaller bird. Canyon Lake was one of the few inland places where the white ibis would come to nest and reproduce. The lake was often a destination for birdwatchers because of this rare idiosyncrasy. The wooden road sign at the top of the hill read, "Canyon Lake—3 miles" and even had a picture of a white ibis painted on it. The lake was only an hour from the ocean, but the ibis usually stayed closer to the temperate salt water where they could feed on small fish and coastal plants. For some reason, the white ibis' were called back to Canyon Lake, year after year, to restart their life cycle. Some would die there and some would give birth to new life at the lake. The ibis poked its head up, looked toward Kennedy briefly, and then went back to plundering the mud with its long, thin beak.

Kennedy heard leaves rustle loudly behind him. He quickly turned to see nothing. He adjusted his glasses and looked about. He saw that all of the people were gone. There were no joggers or fishermen. There were no paired sets of couples staring romantically into each other's eyes. As if instantly, every last person had disappeared. Kennedy was alone.

When he turned back to the water, the white ibis too had departed, leaving only a rapidly fading ripple in the water. He felt a sudden coolness as the temperature began to drop. It dropped quickly. His mind told him that nothing was wrong, but he felt that something was out of place. There was only silence.

Dark clouds the color of gun metal and charcoal quickly converged above him and blotted out the sky. The sweet smell of cedar dissipated as the light wind now brought forth a moldy musk of damp decay. He tossed his papers in the briefcase and quickly snapped it shut.

The first misty vapors began to fall. The lake pushed out a light fog that made a slither sound as it worked its way between the trees and large ferns. The silver air shimmered within the light rain and created a surreal glow that surrounded the lake in the last few minutes of twilight. The cold dampness slapped at his face and hands.

The wind gusted strongly and Kennedy heard a faint whisper. It was barely recognizable; at first he was unsure. He heard it again. It was muffled sounding but clear enough to understand. Someone was calling his name, "Ken—ne—dy." He turned to see the ibis standing in the distance behind him, centered between two large trees. Kennedy ignored the voice and quickly wrote it off to his imagination.

The bird cocked its head to the side and looked at him peculiarly. Kennedy stared into the bird's eyes but saw only vacant black. It was the black of a deep old well and it made him shiver. His body felt colder, chilled, and utterly damp. The bird stared back, expressionless. It seemed to understand something beyond Kennedy's grasp. Kennedy was frozen, lost in the ebony of the perplexingly vacant sockets of the bird's wicked eyes.

The rain intensified and the bird flew off slowly with large swooping flaps, its wings not making a sound. The white ibis faded into the evening fog. The absence of the bird revealed a beautiful young woman in her late twenties, very far off in the distance, much farther away than the ibis had been. She wore a torn white dress, the same white as the ibis. She stood motionless, her arms at her sides, her long blond hair soaked and covering her face. Her skin was slick and she shined a pale blue aura that surrounded her entire body and gleamed back against the fog. She seemed to be nearly transparent.

The bird must have blocked her from my sight, he thought. He stared for a second then called out, "Miss. Can I help you?" There was no response. She stood like a statue. His voice intensified and became slightly shrill, "M'am, do I—I know you? Is there something . . . wrong?"

Without a sound, the woman slowly turned from him and walked away, moving like silk curtains through an open window, her feet gracefully gliding just above the ground. She disappeared into the fog, her bluish glow fading quickly behind her.

Kennedy heard only rain. Strong rain. He pulled his wet hair back off of his glasses for a closer look, but the woman was gone. He looked back toward the parking lot where his car was parked, hoping to see a sign of the woman. He heard no car starting, nor even a horse trotting away up the mountain road. "That's the only way in and out of here," he said to himself. "I should be able to see her." He paused for a few seconds, but saw only dimming light as the night squeezed shades of purple and black that swept rapidly over the lake.

The rain poured. Kennedy turned to the bench, grabbed his briefcase and hurried to the parking lot. Again he scanned for the woman. He called, "Are you there?!" Miss? Hel-looo . . ." There was no response. He pulled his keys out of his front pants pocket, clicked off the alarm to his white BMW sedan and got in to drive home.

The downpour remained constant. The large drops rapped repeatedly against his car's windshield, faster than the blades could shove them off. Kennedy drove home in silence, carefully navigating the twisting road, a road that was twice as dangerous after dark and even more so when the heavy Oregon rains decided to fall. For a few minutes, as he climbed the hill, he continued to look for the woman, knowing that he would have to pass her along the road somewhere even if she was walking.

"What the hell was all that?" He nervously asked but he had no answer. Despite the cold, he felt his own sweat running down his back. It was times like this that he wished he hadn't ever quit smoking. He thought, *yeah, a smoke would do me just fine about now, settle my nerves a bit.* He slowed the car slightly as he approached a sweeping turn, navigated through it perfectly, and then began to talk to himself again. "What was that woman doing over there anyway? Where did she go? Who was she?" He thought something was weird about her. *She just didn't look right. Her skin looked, well, almost translucent.* He was unable to accept that she was anything other than some woman who was either lost or on some sort of drugs or something. His well-trained, analytical mind would somehow find a logical explanation.

"I didn't see her before . . . before . . . that bird!" He felt that cold chill race through his body again. He continued nervously talking to himself. "Those goddamn eyes! They weren't there! Well, they were there, but they weren't . . . *really* there!" He wiped some sweat from his brow and tossed his wet reading glasses on the passenger seat. "It called my name . . . I know it did! Or, she did. Jesus . . . Someone did! I clearly heard a damn voice saying my name!"

Kennedy thought of the girl standing there, looking like she had been forcefully held down in embalming fluid for several days. He thought of that blue shine, but justified it as some sort of an optical illusion from the sunset and the rainy fog. He thought, *isn't that how they explain a lot of U.F.O. sightings? Swamp gas reflecting off of a weather balloon?* He laughed a little at the thought.

He knew that he had to keep his cool. Hearing his own voice began to make him realize just how ridiculous the whole event sounded. It just *couldn't* have happened. There had to be some normal reason for it all. He had read some-where that people under extreme duress could have a form of lucid dreams while they are technically awake, sort of like sleepwalking, except that the person plays an active role in the experience. Sure, that seemed like it could make sense. But, Kennedy knew this experience was different. He wasn't under any particular excessive stress at the moment and he felt very cognizant of his surroundings. In fact, prior to whatever it was that happened, he felt like he had a pretty good bead on things; like his life was heading in the right direction and the world was his oyster. The somnambulistic sleepwalking theory didn't hold water. "I was there! It *did* happen . . . didn't it?"

The BMW's headlights shined against the garage as he pulled into the driveway of his two story home and parked. The rain weakened to a light drizzle. The older home was situated on a decently sized corner lot, but it had only two bedrooms, one of which had been converted into a home of-fice full of hardcover books and paperwork. The front of the house was done in brick and had some ivy, the red and green leaves crawling up at the corners. This was characteristic of the homes in the University or 'U' District, many of which were built before or around the turn of the 20th century. A large pine took up most of the front yard and provided shade on those long, hot summer days, the days when the rains were temporarily all but a memory.

During the last twenty minutes of the forty-five minute drive home from Canyon Lake, he had calmed his nerves, somewhat. He was an educated man and knew that there had to be some reason for what he had gone through, something besides what he thought he saw. *Maybe I've put in too many hours. I should've skipped teaching this summer. I must just be worn out and exhausted.*

He had heard of such things happening to professors in the past. People would talk of hallucinations or hearing things that were there for a second and then they were gone. He always made the joke, "Yeah, I've seen some things too. I think we can thank Dr. Timothy Leary for those apparitions." He knew deep down that this was more than some random flashback, or other stress or drug related experience. He had only taken that particular drug once, when he was an older teenager. He had always opted for the more 'organic' means of recreation. LSD was synthetic, and even then his health was important enough to keep him from doing such harder drugs. Besides, that was the one time when he didn't have control of his situation and surroundings. He had been along for the ride, wherever it took him, good or bad. Luckily, nothing major happened and he had a good 'trip,' watching the colors emanate from the 'Wall of Sound' speakers at the Cow Palace while the air was filled with the sounds of the Grateful Dead playing, "Box of Rain" and "The Wheel" with an extended jam sandwiched in between the two songs. But, as good as the music had been, the LSD experience was not the type of enjoyment that he had ever wanted to recreate.

Kennedy exited the car with his briefcase, walked to the house and grabbed the mail from the black metal box near the front door. Upon entering his well furnished home, he found it empty except for his calico cat. Her name was Emily Dickinson, or Emily for short. He set his briefcase and the mail on the cherry wood kitchen table, and then he leaned down and petted his cat, carefully scratching her outstretched neck. She purred intensely and rubbed her head against his pant leg.

Over a dinner of stir fried teriyaki tofu, steamed broccoli and jasmine rice, he browsed through his mail. He sipped at a half glass of an Australian Shiraz and Cabernet mix, while he looked through the envelopes.

It was the usual junk mail. There were advertisements for grocery store sales, home building items, several different pizza place coupons, a few of them 'take and bake,' medical insurance flyers, cable television and satellite TV deals, and of course flyers for the gardeners and landscapers who claimed that they could beautify and maintain your lawns, in all types of weather, all for a minimal monthly fee. However, there was one exception, one very official looking piece of documentation. Kennedy recognized the gold lettering immediately as coming from the Board of Directors for the University of Oregon. He set down his wineglass and carefully but quickly opened it. The letter read:

Dear Kennedy Jones, PhD.

We are pleased to welcome you to the University of Oregon, Board of Regents and Order of Educators, as a fully tenured professor. This employment promotion is effective immediately and will include a substantial increase in wage and benefits, the details of which are to follow in a later correspondence.

You are hereby granted full tenure, with all of the rights and privileges associated as such. Congratulations on all of your hard work and extra effort over the past five years. Our entire committee excitedly sends you our best wishes in this new phase of your career.

Our office will be in touch with you soon with information regarding the official presentation of your certificate of achievement. Please do not hesitate to contact us for any reason before that time with any questions that you might have. Again, congratulations!

Very Truly Yours:
Franklin S. Salazar, PhD, JD, Dean of University Administration

Kennedy jumped up, threw his hands in the air and let out a scream of "Whoo-hoo!" that startled Emily. He quickly picked her up and danced around the kitchen with her, the whole time clutching the letter. He set her down on the floor and said, "This is cause for celebration" as he uncorked a bottle of Dom Perignon champagne that had been waiting in his refrigerator for just that moment. He filled a tall flute, then walked over to the stereo and turned on a classical CD. It was Handel's "Water Music." That had always been his favorite collection to listen to when he just wanted to be at peace and enjoy the space.

After filling Emily a bowl of salmon pate, her special treat for the occasion, he kicked off his shoes and then flopped down on his couch and crossed his feet onto the coffee table. The calm music began to sweetly serenade him. He was feeling quite content. He stared around his living room, seeing a few small, tasteful sculptures, some ironwood carvings that he had picked up on one of his trips driving down to the Sea of Cortez in Mexico, and some classic looking paintings on the walls. One was a giclee replica of Monet's "Water Lilies," framed in a deep red wood and matted with aged silver trim. Emily jumped up onto his lap and momentarily startled him, until she immediately began to purr. He briefly scratched just behind her ears, and then she cleaned herself contently, having just finished her very rich special snack.

After finishing the entire bottle of champagne over the course of an hour, and briefly passing out on the couch, Kennedy got up and clicked the remote to turn off the music which had just restarted. He ventured forward, lifting his now heavy legs and stumbling a little. His vision blurred slightly, and then it readjusted to the light. He headed to the kitchen, grabbed a tall glass of water and two small round ibuprofen pills. He figured he was better safe than sorry. At the foot of the staircase, he downed the pills with a large gulp just before he made the climb up the stairs with the rest of his glass of water.

Kennedy entered his bedroom. He walked over and pulled open the intricately patterned curtains with his free hand, revealing a full moon through the large window. The late summer skies were often clear at night, especially after a hard rain. He lifted up the painted wood pane to allow for some fresh night air to ease its way in. His body temperature had elevated with the champagne still circulating through his system, and the coolness felt soothing.

The white light through the clear night air was crisp and it allowed him to maneuver back to the bed easily. He sat down, took a big swig of water, swallowed hard, and set the now halfway empty glass on the nightstand. He pulled off his shirt and pants, then his white undershirt, careless of where they landed. He fell back hard onto the bed without pulling any covers over him. He was immediately asleep.

CHAPTER 4

A handsome young man sat behind a large desk in a medical imaging facility. He was one of four busy receptionists. The desk was stained oak and resembled an elongated half moon with squared off edges. It had a raised front counter, with a signature sheet at the end nearest the front doors. Behind the countertop was a lower desk area that housed the computer screens, miscellaneous medical forms and the standard office supplies like paperclips, pens, highlighters, staplers, tape dispensers and lined yellow sticky pads.

The man wore black slacks and a red polo shirt that matched the three other receptionist's shirts. His coworkers were all women. On the left side of his shirt, just to the side of the buttons on the collar, was a name tag that read, "Medical Imaging Center" in large white letters against a black background, and in much smaller letters, "Reception." There was his picture on it. In it, he was clean shaven and had much shorter hair than he did currently. The picture represented his 'looking for a job' look, which meant completely 'clean cut.' The name on his identification tag was, "Dave." Of course, last names were once used but in the modern age of stalkers and lawsuits, people doing business, especially hospital business, remained on a first name only basis. It was only to be the information given that was absolutely necessary in order to perform the required job at hand.

David Jones stared blankly at the computer terminal in front of him, the bluish and green light reflecting back at him. His area was nearest the doors, at the end of the desk; pole position. He was the first defense against the onslaught of sick and dying patients. This place where he always sat was the most dreaded place to sit, because one had to greet everyone that came through the door, as well as keep the flow of patients moving through for their exams. For some people, this reception position would have been a great long term job to land. It was a Monday through Friday work week, had good benefits, offered a decent wage, and the workplace was an indoor, office environment. But this was not true for Dave. He often thought, *what the hell am I still doing here?*

Dave sighed, then got up and leaned over the countertop, looking at the sign in sheet for the next name on the list, last name first of course. Apparently, it was okay for the patients to use full last and first names, because of their being within the context of a hospital situation and environment. A few people, patients and staff, had brought up the hypocritical privacy issues regarding signatures to the imaging center's administration in the past; however, the superiors had deemed that their procedures were still safe. The Health Insurance Portability and Accountability Act or 'HIPPA' guidelines were yet to become a hard reality for the medical community at large. They knew it was coming down the pike, but for now it was status quo, business as usual.

Dave crossed out the name with a black Sharpie pen, and then he sat back into his chair. He looked up over his computer screen, out toward the sardine can of people in the lobby and called out, "Vasquez." Then slightly louder, "Frances—Vasquez," being sure to pronounce the last name with the hard "K" sound instead of the "QU" sound that most Americans would utter. He had taken more than three years of university level Spanish, and accelerated in them, during his Bachelor's degree. He thought, *a lot of good my Journalism Bachelor's degree has done me. I still can't find a better job than herding patients through a human organ and bone Xerox center . . . my job consists of being kind of like a Kinko's for people's insides.*

Dave had completed his degree two years ago and there hadn't been a lot of opportunities in this predominantly white community to use his Spanish language knowledge outside of school. Because of this, he had gotten rusty. So, he rarely chose to address the Spanish speaking patients with anything other than English. On occasion, he would surprise the other receptionists by conversing in Spanish with a patient, but it was only the bare minimum to get that person checked in for his or her exam. Dave would say many "lo siento" or "I'm sorry" statements during the course of their exchanges. Generally, the patients appreciated his efforts.

One particular coworker, Candy, a petite lady in her fifties with died jet black and heavily hair sprayed hair, long fake fingernails and tons of costume jewelry, was always very nice to him. She had worked for the imaging company for over 15 years. She was a lifer. She'd come up and pat Dave on the back when he was done "interpreting" and say, "My Davey, you handled that very well. I wish I could speak another language." Then, she'd cross off the next name on the list with the black pen and go back to her seat on the opposite end of the desk. With that much time in on any job, there were some advantages. For instance, she was able to sit the farthest away from the flurry as possible, sort of like Generals in the military, but without all of the clout. Her shy sounding, squeaky little voice would call out to the patients, "Mis-ter Flan-a-gan . . ."

Once, Dave had played a joke on her when there were very few people in the lobby. It was late in the afternoon. He had seen Candy was next in line to call for a patient and that she was finishing up some paperwork, so he quickly grabbed the list and wrote, "Man, Spider" on it in cursive, and then he sat back down. Candy got up and crossed the name off, calling, "Mis-ter . . . Man . . . Spi-der Man," then she quickly turned to Dave with a comical look of being upset upon realizing what she had said. The other receptionists, Betty and Dana, laughed to themselves. Even one of the patients who heard it let out a small chuckle from behind the Sunset magazine that he was reading while he waited for his abdominal ultrasound.

With Dave's subtle smirk and stifled laughter, it was obvious who had performed the prank. Candy knew that the joke was harmless and that he had finally called her on her repetitious nature of get up, call the name, sit down and check them in; auto-pilot. After all, she was just doing her time now. There was no gold watch at the end of this rainbow. With fifteen years at this same redundant, "keep up the pace and don't think" job, she had programmed herself very well.

She just tipped her glasses a little, the rhinestones reflecting the fluorescent lights, then came over and gave him a good fake choking. She said, "Oh you, Davey . . ."

"Davey;" He hated that name. It reminded him of some childish, eternally boyish looking fellow who sang for a Sixties musical group, and all of the young adolescent and pre-adolescent girls would fawn over him and squeal when he entered the room. Not even when he was young would he allow that name to be used in reference to him. But, he liked Candy in a grandmother sort of way, so he let her and only her, call him Davey. Actually, he preferred David but opted for Dave since he'd used it most of his life. His mother had wanted to call him Sebastian but his father liked David better. Eventually, Dave realized how glad he was not to have been named Sebastian. It sounded too rich boy preppie for him when he was a kid growing up just outside of Oakland, California. *That's a name that'll get your ass kicked, and quick.* So, Dave it was.

The hum of the building was nearly deafening, but nobody noticed. The people just talked louder, projecting their voices over the television blaring "The Price is Right," or the CT, MRI and Ultrasound machines down the hall, as well as the background Muzak that belched out hits from the 1970s and 1980s that had been turned into some kind of monotonous, instrumental, less than acceptable lounge versions of their original compositions. Of course, most of the doctors would hum along to the songs as if they couldn't tell the difference between voiceless renditions and the original recordings. In their defense, most of their brain cells were spent focusing on more concrete concerns, and for the patients that was sometimes a very good thing.

The patients themselves, many of them elderly and hard of hearing to begin with, made it more difficult to hear because of their long drawn out stories, told at full volume in the lobby, about whose grandkids did something special last weekend or some new ailment that hadn't killed them yet, but *could* kill them at any time. These facts absolutely had to be shared with anyone else in the room who would listen. Many of the patients were dying and proud of whatever crazy thing that was killing them. There is a certain pride in being a survivor. Whether the illness was due to smoking, living next to an electrical substation for years, skin cancer from over exposure to the sun because of a decreased Ozone layer, drinking overly fluoridated water full of Chlorine, eating GEI based food grown with the use of RBGH, DDT, Benzene, Sodium Nitrates and Nitrites, cyanide or any other form of chemically 'enhancing' products, the results were nearly always the same. There was to be cancer of some kind leading them to terminal conditions. Even with all of the marvels of modern, Western medical science, no one had been able to stop those unusable cells from replicating. So, the patients kept coming in for their given diagnosis, based on imaging procedures. Of course, the irony was that the radiation from imaging procedures damaged the body and could even cause cancer itself. But sometimes we hope that the end result justifies the means and that the risks that we take outweigh the potential consequences.

The patient's discussions often seemed like a competition of who could get worse and still live: "my kidney is . . ." followed by, "that ain't nuttin', you got two of 'dem. My liver is shot, and I gots this a-here tingy wid my lungs . . . I think dey called it a nod-jule . . ." Dave didn't understand it. He didn't know how they could just go on about it, like it was a source of pride. He thought, *don't they realize that they're dying?*

Dave remembered when he was six years old and still living in a rural East Coast town. This was a time when his Great Grandfather, Henry, had been hit with cancer from years of smoking Pall Mall non-filter cigarettes. Even at six, Dave had realized how helpless he was and how this disease rapidly debilitated his favorite relative. Henry had stood close to six foot four and was an in shape looking man, from his many years of working in the fields of his parents' and then his own farm.

Henry had always been a hard worker and for a short time he had taken a job with General Motors that included a lease car and many benefits as well; however, in the long run, it only lasted a few years. His heart was in farming and living closer to the cycles of the land. Henry used to say, "What the hell do we need cars for when we've gotten around on horses just fine for so many years?" That was the kind of man he was, one of the old school, back to basics types.

Henry and Dave had had a special relationship. David was the oldest of all of the great grandchildren and incidentally the only one who would later still have vivid memories of Henry. Dave's family, Henry included, all grew up way too fast, and began having children when they were still nearly children themselves. That was part of why Dave got to know his great grandfather for a few years, when most families do not have this luxury. When Dave was born, his great, great grandfather was still alive for more than a year. Dave knew that someone a long time ago, maybe it was his mom, had shown him a picture of him as a baby and the others that made up a five generation family picture. Of course, Dave and his mother had left Upstate New York early and he hadn't followed that route of early family procreation. Dave had never been married and he had no children of his own.

Most of the girls in that area of New York had their first child between fourteen and sixteen years old, some even younger, and nobody thought anything of it. When people grew up in such a poor community and they were not educated about sex, unless it was to be told 'don't do it' or 'just say no,' things tended to happen that way, generation after generation after generation.

Dave remembered one occasion, when Henry was just getting sick. His great grandfather called young David away from his Legos to talk to him, away from the other children. Henry leaned out from the door, standing on the top stair of the staircase that led down to the cellar.

"David. Come here, be quiet and come on over here son, into the cellar."

"What Grandpa?"

"Hurry, I've somethin' for ya. Don't let the other kids know." David dropped his plastic toys and quietly but quickly walked over to his great grandfather.

"David, come down here. Close the door softly behind you." Dave did just that, following Henry down the stairs to where they ended at the cement cellar floor. Henry reached up and pulled on a thin chain that hung from the ceiling, turning on the exposed light bulb. He leaned down and spoke softly into David's ear. "I wanted you to have something, because you're the oldest. It wouldn't mean as much to the others."

David was intrigued, wondering what this big secret was all about. Henry rarely spoke to the children with more than a 'hello' or 'stay out of the study'. He wasn't a mean man and could actually be very affectionate. But usually he was a stereotypical farmer, a man of few words. David asked, "Grandpa, what is it?"

Henry answered, "Here" and he handed young David a wallet. "Yur the oldist, and the oldist always have it the toughist." He paused briefly then continued, "maybe, ita gib ya a diffrent perspective. I was the oldist and coulda used a break or two when I was a youngun."

The wallet was brand new and made of dark brown leather. It had petite, fine leather stitching around the edges. David grabbed it and looked at it in awe. He had never seen anything so nice with such time, effort and craftsmanship put into it. This wallet had not been made by a machine, but judging by the quality it could have been, only it was put together better than any machine ever could have made it. David felt the soft rigidness of the smooth leather with his thumb.

David whispered, trying to keep the air of being clandestine, "Wow." After a few moments, he opened the wallet and saw that it contained a ten dollar bill. Henry had already stood up and began to turn toward the stairs again. David looked up and saw his great grandfather, standing there in blue jeans and a flannel shirt, still looking majestic. He said, "Grandpa . . . you forgot your money . . . in here . . ."

Henry smiled at the innocence of the boy, at the honesty that some children have at least for awhile. It warmed Henry's heart to see such a young person, so naïve, so untouched by the greed of the older people's world and the world at large, so willing to do the right thing. Henry replied quietly, "No, no, son, that's fer you."

"For me?" David's voice sounded almost like a mouse squeak.

"Like I said, the oldist have it the toughist. Maybe someday you'll look back on this, when the tings ain't goin' so good, and you'd remember whud it is I'm a sayin' to ya." Henry reached down and patted young David on the back affectionately. David smelled the comforting scent of the cigarettes mixed with Old Spice cologne. He looked up into his great grandfather's eyes, those ice blue eyes that had seen at least an entire lifetime. "David, run along upstairs with the others, and don't' say nuthin' about this, 'kay?" His great grandfather smiled, and his sun hardened wrinkles seemed to soften slightly for a moment.

"Oh, I won't grandpa, I won't."

That was the last really good memory that Dave had of his great grandfather. It was just before the cancer began to eat Henry alive and took him away slowly over the next year.

The fluorescent hospital lights hummed steadily in the waiting room of the imaging center. An elderly Hispanic woman approached Dave's fenced in area of the desk. There were wooden separators between each of the receptionists that stopped just behind the upper counter of the desk. They were supposed to create a sense of privacy, sort of an individual workspace area. Dave remembered that they had been installed the previous year because of the upcoming 'HIPPA' regulations regarding privacy and patient information. They were a joke; clear glass windows in between each of the areas. Anyone could see anyone else's information, they just needed to turn their head. And, all the privacy that they were supposed to afford was nullified by the receptionists having to practically yell over each other at the desk just so that the person in front of him or her could hear the registration questions. Even then, the elderly patients, of which there were many, would answer with an "uh, huh" or "yup" when they clearly hadn't even heard or understood the question.

The lady at the counter, Mz. Vasquez, stopped directly in front of him and said, "good morning, David" in a soothingly pleasant voice. It was a voice that had fought for several years to suppress the fact that she came to The United States, Los Estados Unidos, from Mexico when she was in her late twenties. Due to her strict Catholic upbringing, although she was not so strict to the faith these days, she was usually very formal to everyone in business or other professional settings. She would call him David, even though his nametag read 'Dave'.

"Good morning, David."

"Hello, Mrs. Vasquez."

"Um, I, I prefer Frances . . . especially since my husband passed on a few months ago . . . if you don't mind, Sir." This struck Dave as a little odd, especially since she had just been so formal sounding with his name. *Calling me Sir? I'm half her age.*

Dave had recognized her from the past two years or so. She would come in with her husband Enrique, who was diagnosed as terminal. Frances had been trying hard to accept her husband's recent death. Enrique had died after a long battle with melanoma. The two of them had been in several times for X-rays, MRIs, CTs . . . you name it. All of the information and testing just came to the same results. He was going to die. For that two year period, It hadn't been if anymore, it was only when. Dave felt a twinge of humanity laced with mortality nip at his brain. He thought, *Her husband wasn't that old. Fifty-seven, if I remember right. Man, that is too young to go.*

"No problem, whatever you're comfortable with, Frances." Dave returned to his work. "You're here for a mammogram, right?" She nodded. He smiled a smile that could have been confused more for flirting rather than kindness. She smiled back. He continued, "Oh, and I am very sorry to hear about your husband. He seemed like a very nice man from the little that I knew of him."

She looked for a brief second if she would cry, but it was a subtle look and one less perceptive than Dave would not have normally noticed. Then, she composed herself very quickly and said, "Thank you." After a brief pause where she was thinking of how to phrase something she said, "he *is* a good man. He lived three lifetimes in his fifty-seven years, and he helped to raise four beautiful children to become successful, compassionate adults." Dave felt a little like he might have said something wrong. "Enrique, my Eric, used to fish and paint the most beautiful seascapes. He was always at home near the water . . ." She stopped, took a deep breath and this time did wipe the faintest hint of a tear from the corner of her eye. "I miss him dearly, but I know that I'll see him again, soon enough." She looked up to Dave, seemingly seeking approval for her comments. He kept his smile up, although it was growing a little stale. "That's how it is with true love. You're never really apart for very long."

Dave was taken back for a moment, but this type of thing happened to him very regularly. For some reason, partially because of the context of his job, and partially because he had the type of personality that allowed for such interactions, perfect strangers would open up to him and reveal the most intimate aspects of their lives.

Dave had often thought of himself as an underpaid imaging center bartender: the receptacle of all the patients' unwanted hang-ups, idiosyncrasies and problems. On one occasion, an elderly lady patient had even told him that she was leaving her husband of 26 years for another woman. "Yup, I like women. I'm a Lesbian and proud of it." There wasn't much that could startle him after doing this job for over four years, two years of which were during his degree and the rest since his graduating. *Stuck with this job, and all the associated baggage.*

"I'm sorry if I offended you, Misses, um, I mean, Frances. I meant neither you nor your husband any disrespect. I wish I could have known him better."

"None taken. I guess I am still getting used to all of this." After a pause and a refreshing smile she said, "Do you have someone special in your life, David?" He raised his eyebrows and got a slightly curious look on his face. "Oh, David, I'm sorry, I'm prying."

Dave continued to fill in the paperwork, glancing back and forth to the computer screen. He stopped and said, "No, no, it's fine. I do have a fiancé. Christy is her name." He glanced quickly at the list that was now piling up with names. When he wasn't spending additional time checking in a patient, he could almost double the volume of patients that the other receptionists were checking in. This was even true of Candy, although she worked very solidly and methodically and had been able to create a groove for herself that paced her well throughout the day. She remained fresh and she rarely got tired. Candy's knowledge gathered over the years more than made up for her slightly reduced speed. And, she also never seemed to get stressed.

Dave continued, "We're to be married . . ." and now whispering, "as soon as I can find a real job." He laughed a little, but she could see the resentment he held for being nearly 30, although he only looked 22, and still working at the imaging center.

Frances, also whispering, leaned over the counter close to his ear and answered, "You can't put your life on hold for something as silly as a job. Jobs are a way to make money . . . a necessity. We work because we have to. Some people love their work, some hate their work and love their life, and a few lucky people love both. Jobs don't define your entire life, or at least, they shouldn't." Her expression grew a little more serious. "What if your *real job* never comes? Then what? You might just lose what is most important to you." She looked down at the counter, feeling like she might have crossed the line and gotten too philosophical. Then, she looked back into his eyes and said, "Do you love her? I mean, is she the one?"

"Of course I do, she is, it's just . . ." The check in list was now on to a second page. That was always bad news. Frances saw him look at the page again and got the hint. She stood back upright and without being coarse, she resumed the patient and caregiver posture of medical office professionalism.

"David, please think about what I said. We're all put on this Earth to learn something before moving on, so we don't have to do it all over again. I mean, if you believe in that sort of thing." She smiled and said, "I sure do."

Dave finished checking her in and handed her the appropriate forms with a clipboard. He gave her the obligatory, "good to see you. Take care, Frances." After a moment, as she was walking away toward a seat he continued, "Hopefully, the next time I see you will be outside the hospital."

She chuckled, understanding what he meant. "Young man, let's hope you're right." She walked over and sat down next to a table with a small reading lamp on it and began to fill out her part of the paperwork. The noise continued.

"I've had three knee replacements . . . this one's a ti-tanium one."

"Three?! Try four . . . two on each side! Well, I ain't got the newer one yet like you, though."

Dave thought to himself, *does she really believe in that shit? That born again sort of thing? Or even, the die and go to heaven deal? Some great reward for a life of misery? Some reason to perform subservient service to the condescending higher power? You pay your dues and then move up the religious ladder to Heaven? Like a spiritual cash machine or something? Nice thinking. Whatever gets them from one Sunday to the next.* Dave stared at Frances for another moment. He actually was thinking about what she said.

"Hey, Dave. Dave. Dave! There's people on the list." It was Betty. Her real name was Elizabeth, but she preferred to go by Betty. She had only been there for six months but had worked in other medical facilities, dentist's and optician's offices, so she had an understanding of the job. However, she had never previously had to keep pace with checking in between three and four hundred exams in any given day.

The pressure was getting to her, but she did her best to cover it up. She was as sickly sweet as a pecan pie, so no one really saw through her facade. No one really cared. She showed up to work early every day and always was the first to volunteer to work extra shifts. Dave wrote that off to her being 20 years old, overly and outwardly religious, and not desiring to ever do anything more with her life. This was God's plan for her and it suited her just fine. *She's probably not smart enough to do anything else*, he thought. In reality, she was fairly bright and just happened to be very devout to her faith.

Dave didn't like her, but he had to play the work game because she sat next to him for eight or more hours, five days a week. She was an overall good person, as were most of the workers at the imaging center. But, Dave often had problems with seeing the good in people, especially when it came to coworkers in a job that he was not happy with. When he picked them apart, he was really just projecting his own, self imposed humiliation and inner frustration with his situation. It's much easier to discredit others than to fix yourself.

"Yeah Betty, I got it." He noticed that Dana had disappeared again. Whenever the crowd remained too steady for too long, it was spontaneous break time for her. Each receptionist was allowed two, ten minute breaks a day and one half hour lunch. Dana took more than three times that many breaks, if you count the times that she was off pretending to work, carrying around a piece of paper on a clip board and walking from department to department, bullshitting and talking about irrelevant things with whomever would listen, and the whole time trying to look busy and happy to any passing superiors.

Oh, and then there were her smoke breaks that didn't seem to figure in to the schedule. She would say, "I need a puff," followed by, "you don't understand what it is like to be addicted to something like this . . . I've tried to quit." Then she would just leave, no matter how busy it was, grabbing her leather Harley Davidson purse. Her straight, waist length gray hair would flip out to the side and her large chest would bounce beneath her too tight polo work shirt, as she quickly scuttled past. You could tell that she was pretty once, many cigarettes ago.

Dana would just be sitting there one minute and then "poof," she was gone. Dave speculated that at times she was hiding back in the storage closet, or in the lounge room, having a cup of coffee and telling herself that she could make it through the day. "I think I can . . . I think I can . . . chug, chug, chug."

Dana had her own problems having been left by her husband, with a mortgage and kids to tend to on her own. He left her a note one day when he was supposed to be going to his welding job. It said, "It's been fun, but I gotta go. I'll call when I get to where I'm going." That was the last she heard of him, four years ago. Most people would have felt sorry for her, had they known her situation, but not Dave, at least not in his current self absorbed mental funk.

Dave leaned over and crossed off another name on the list, speaking with the repetitiveness of a macaw parrot, "Hi. Please sign in and we'll call you up in just a few minutes." People still piled in and formed a line that nearly went back out the door. *I've said this how many times now? One million? Maybe two?*

After a few hours, it finally slowed down. It was nearly twelve thirty in the afternoon and most of the referring physician's offices would be closed until one thirty. *They* all could take an hour and a half for lunch, just shut the place down. He thought sarcastically, *people actually close down an office and give everyone the same lunch time? What an amazing concept!*

Dave and Candy were the only ones that remained sitting behind the desk. Dana had eventually had to go home because one of her two kids, both of them girls in their twenties, single and still living at home, had locked herself out of the house. Because it was a half hour drive from Eugene to outside of Cottage Grove, she took the rest of the day off. *Figures.* Betty had gone to lunch, since Candy had just returned. Betty had told Candy that she would be a little late coming back because she had to run home for something herself. But, she assured her that she would be back. Candy always went to lunch first. Seniority does have its privileges.

Dave always took his lunch last since he came in at 9:30am and had to work the latest day shift. It made sense and many people would have liked to have the late lunch to make the rest of the day seem to go by more quickly. However, lately, Dave was focused on the negative in both his coworkers and his job and therefore he could not see the good in either one of them.

Even though Dave had seniority second only to Candy, his shift had remained the later one. He had spoken to his supervisor, Rochelle, but to no avail. She always said that she needed him to "close up the shop" because he was "so good at it" and it would be too hard to train someone else to do it. He knew the night shift, as well as the day shift, so he could close out and prepare everything for the slower pace of the evening. Not that there weren't a million things to do at night: catching up paperwork, filing charts, stocking the exam rooms, making coffee and making sure that the office was prepared for the next day's worth of voluminous patients. But, there were much fewer patients and all of the managers and most of the doctors went home in the evening. At night, Dave used to work with one janitor and two to three technologists at the most. Often, there was just one MRI tech who took emergency calls from the hospital. It was the same set up on the weekends, of which Dave had put in many hours of work.

That is the thing that he missed the most about the night shift, the freedom from authority and constant supervision. The faster morning pace wasn't so bad; it made the time go by quickly. But there were too many negatives for him to really make it an enjoyable job. And, any job that paid that poorly should have at least been fun.

Along with coming in later and closing out the front desk, there came the duty of sitting in the hell seat next to the sign in sheet. When you come in last, you have to take what is left. And, no one ever sat in that seat intentionally. If for some reason he had switched shifts to come in earlier and cover for another receptionist, Rochelle made sure that he still sat in that first seat nearest the entryway. She probably had her legitimate reasons, but Dave always viewed it as an enactment of her prejudices and resulting power plays toward him.

He often thought of complaining to the higher ups about Rochelle. He had trained her as a receptionist while he was still going to school. She had since taken on the newly created "Reception Supervisor" position. She had even tried to change the reception position name to "Registrationist" so as to encompass a wider variety of duties, (downsizing in action) but had failed thus far to push it through. Rochelle had been with the company a year less than he, but her nose was a much darker shade of brown. Dave thought that she was intimidated by his intelligence, education, and natural flair for customer service. He was probably right to some extent. Besides, he was a guy . . . a guy who had grown up in the large, culturally diverse metropolitan Bay Area of San Francisco and Rochelle was a very local, small town Oregon girl with land rich parents that had given her and her husband 20 acres just outside of town. It was their wedding gift. Dave would never see such generosity from his family.

It seemed perfectly okay for Rochelle to give vacation days to the other workers with less seniority than him; they were women. And, this was probably to be the job that they each would retire from, provided the company kept them that long. Rochelle knew that Dave would eventually leave his position, and she played that up every chance she could. It wasn't really fair, but there was not much that he could do about it. He was over qualified for the position, that is true, but when there are no other prospects available, you take what you can get and you keep it. There was no way that Dave could ever prove her favoritism toward the others, especially her absolute favorite Betty, and he knew that. So, it was again just a matter of putting on the game face and dealing with the situation as best he could.

Outside of the imaging center, Rochelle was a great mother and she had a great relationship with her husband as well. Her family was always bright eyed and happy when they came in to visit her or to take her to lunch. Dave saw this, but still viewed her as vindictive and self serving. Maybe if they had met outside of work, he might have actually liked her. She was a good person, just trying to do her job the best that she knew how to.

Dave grabbed a stack of letters to be folded and a handful of preprinted business envelopes. Candy did the same. They had worked very hard that morning and deserved a break, but that was not Rochelle's style. There was no earning of downtime. That would have been considered inefficiency. If a higher up came by and saw idleness, Rochelle would be to blame and everyone knows that shit runs downhill. You really couldn't blame her, but it made Dave's job a little tougher. People who have never had to do highly paced work with the public, especially in the medical field, do not understand the stress of constantly interacting with sometimes hostile patients. Every once in awhile, people need a break to recharge and stay on their game.

Dave saw Rochelle sitting in the corner of the room, hidden behind her computer screen, the only person with a new flat screen, and he viewed her as a sort of overlord. If any of the receptionists were idle for too long, or chose to talk to each other for too long, then she would begin to divvy out work to them; the work that no one wanted to do. Dave had figured out long ago that it was better to occupy yourself than to wait for her venomous strike.

As they folded, they spoke softly so as not to attract Rochelle's attention. "Dave."

"Yeah."

"That one lady nearly talked your ear off. What did she want?"

"Oh, not too much. She told me that her husband had died a little bit ago." He paused and looked toward the door to check for patients. Having not seen any, he continued. "They had to come in here a lot over the past few years, so I kinda got to know her a little. You know how it is."

"I thought that she looked familiar. I think I waited on her before."

He laughed a little, "Waited on her? What'd she have a ham and cheese? Any fries? Did she leave you a good tip, also?"

"Okay smart ass, I reg-i-stra-tion-ized her." She too enjoyed a laugh. Candy really liked working with Dave. He had always found a way to make her laugh. He was like the son that she never had. Both of her kids were now full grown and married. Besides, they were girls. However, they each called her at work at least once per day. Candy would huddle over her phone in the corner, nearly whispering, so that it was not so apparent that she was on a personal call. They were all very close. They seemed more like best friends than mother and daughters. Their relationship was a special one.

Candy recalled one time when she had been voted by the rest of the workers of the company as "Employee of the Month." Actually, she was the first one. She was January. There was a large plaque that was to hold the twelve pictures of the corresponding month's recipients, to be changed out at year's end. The plaque had gaudy gold lettering across the top, compliments of Human Resources that said, "MEDICAL IMAGING CENTER. EMPLOYEE OF THE MONTH." And in smaller but equally as obnoxious lettering at the bottom of the frame it said, "Every Single Image Depicts a Tale." Once Candy's picture was put into the frame and hung up on the wall, she was embarrassed by the cheesiness of it. Sure, she wore costume jewelry, fake stones, and sort of loud business attire, but it was completely intentional.

That was her chosen style. She was originally from Southern California, near Beverly Hills, and she could easily recognize when something just wasn't done right. Loud and gaudy had a style to it when it was done correctly, and this is how she chose to express herself.

Although it was a sort of honor to be recognized for her work, Candy had expressed her discontent quietly to Dave, but to no one else. She didn't want to rock the boat. She was shy by nature, but could really chatter your ear off once you got to know her.

That particular day, Dave had an idea. Without letting Candy see him do it, he grabbed a piece of paper and drew a large spiky haired looking wig that was the perfect size for Candy's picture in the encasement. He proceeded to color it in with a fluorescent pink highlighter pen. He used red handled scissors to cut it out, carefully maintaining each spike. He next cut a round half circle underneath the hair so it could easily mount over someone's head and look like "hair."

Dave peeled off a small piece of scotch tape from the holder, rolled it up into a circle, and attached it to the back of the pseudo hair. When Candy had left the desk to dress a patient, he fixed the hair above her face in the picture, sticking the paper wig to the outside glass of the plaque, perfectly surrounding her head. He quickly sat back down and waited.

On her way back to the desk from the dressing room, something caught her attention. Candy glanced over at Human Resource's worker shrine. It took a minute, but then she saw what he had done. She covered her mouth to keep from bursting out in laughter. She hurried back and sat down, saying, "That is just perfect. Oh my God, that is so funny, Davey."

"What are you two talking about?" a voice said.

"Dana, Betty, look what Dave did. Over there, on the Employee of the Month thingy."

They both looked over and got up to take a closer look. Then the laughter began. Dana was less than subtle, an attribute of being raised as a party girl from the early Seventies (get your motor runnin'). Betty was trying to maintain her sweet demeanor, but she too was having a hard time. Even Rochelle got a kick out of the picture when she walked by. However, she insisted that the wig be removed, in the interest of the patients and administration. She pulled it off and threw it in the trash, all without missing a step down the hallway toward the MRI room. Rochelle did actually say, "That was a pretty good one, you guys."

It wasn't until the next day, long after the paper wig had been removed, that there was a general email sent out to the entire company. It read as follows:

> *Employees:*
> *Due to the events of recent days there is an issue that needs to be addressed. There will be no more defacing of the "Employee of the Month" plaque, or any other piece of property on the Medical Imaging Premises.*
>
> *This is unprofessional and is not at all acceptable. We are running a medical office. Such insubordination will not be tolerated and will be punished at least with the perpetrator being written up . . . and probably suspended from work for at least a day. This is to be considered a formal written warning. We are appalled at the childishness of this internal act of vandalism.*
>
> *Regards,*
> *Human Resources*

Everyone knew that the letter was directed toward Dave. Most people had found it funny, a sort of stress reliever for a few minutes. Some people were upset that they hadn't had the chance to see it. It was mainly the night crew; they always got information second or third hand and were completely forgotten about when it came to special celebration days that involved ordering out for food. The best thing that they could hope for, in so far as food or information, would be well picked over and very cold leftovers.

Dave had worked on the night shift until completing his degree, so he knew the routine all too well. He then opted for the day shift so he could live more like a 'normal' human being. He used to sing to himself the famous Bob Dylan line, "Twenty years of schooling and they put you on the day shift." At times, when he was getting ready to go home in the late afternoon, he felt bad for switching shifts. It was like he had deserted his evening coworkers and become one of . . . *them.*

There was one specific person who obviously wasn't amused by his employee of the month tomfoolery. That person was the founder and creator the Employee of the Month idea, the head of Human Resources. Janet. Janet was overweight, short and fifty three years old. Her hair was shoulder length and lifeless and hugged her round freckled cheeks. She dressed in nice, but outdated business attire that fit too tightly, usually two piece suits. This was of course when she was not wearing a Mickey Mouse shirt or some other form of Disney paraphernalia. She was a freak about Disney and both her and her teenage daughter made the pilgrimage to the "American Mecca" in Orlando, Florida at least once per year.

Janet was someone who had climbed up through the ranks, previously managing a large gas station. She had her Associates Degree in Human Resources Management, but did little to help the employees that fell beneath Management status. Basically, her job was to lessen the blow when the Board of Directors made some sort of cuts to benefits, bonuses, or staffing in general, in search of even more millions of dollars in profits. She was the corporate spin doctor, and to those who wanted to believe it, she was quite good at it.

She had had it hard after her daughter was born. Her husband had been killed in a freak military training accident when he was hit by a stray grenade in the Nevada desert. Prior to that, she had been very easy going. But, once that happened she took the attitude that it was her and her daughter against the world. She never remarried and really didn't even date, which could have had something to do with her being perceived as the perennial hard ass. There were times that she was quite tender and loving, but those never came through at work, especially in Dave's eyes. No, to him she was the mechanistic cog overseer with a loaded whip.

Janet took great offense to someone making light of her beautiful plaque. She had taken a long time, looking through catalogs and phoning trophy and award makers, before she decided on just the right look that fit into the Center's corporate image, and of course the budget. She was probably the only one who didn't know for sure that Dave had orchestrated the 'spiked-hair incident' as it came to be called, but it didn't matter. Janet had put her foot down and had made a new precedent. There would be no screwing around at work, even if it was harmless. Although Dave would not be able to "deface" anything at work again, the techs and even one radiologist occasionally would bring up how funny Candy looked with a pink, spiky mop atop her head. "You'd of thought that shy little lady had gone punk or something."

The folding of letters continued for the two of them. The contents were mainly past due statements to patients. Candy searched for small talk. "Dave, so, are you still thinking about going back to school?" She continued to fold the letters and place them in the envelopes with the Medical Imaging Centers logo printed in the space for the return address. Her folds were exactly the same. Perfect. The process had become thoughtless and automatic.

"Well, I'm checking out a doctorate program here at the University." He thought, *Once a Duck, always a Duck.*

"Oh, real-ly." Her voice sounded overly enthusiastic and impressed, but sincere at the same time. No one in her family had gone to anything more that a training seminar, let alone completed any university studies. "What's your degree in again?"

"Journalism and Communications."

"So, you write a lot?" Her understanding of journalism stopped there. There were people who could write, and they studied Journalism or English. There were Math and Science people who became engineers, and then there were doctors and lawyers who were really smart, went to school forever, and made a lot of money. In some respects, the simplifications were correct.

Dave replied, "Yeah, I've written a screenplay and some short stories." He looked toward the door, still no one coming through that would require his services, so he continued. "I haven't been able to publish anything yet, and the job opportunities are very slim around this town. I've been thinking of moving up to Portla . . ."

She cut him off and playfully slapped at his shoulder, "Oh honey, I'm sure that you'll find something soon. You're so smart, and educated . . . I can't believe that you've been here as long as you've been here."

"You and me both, Candy."

Dave felt the sting of reality set in. He had been there for over four years now. He was still making crumby wages but had benefits, although they cost more and covered less each year. He had put off getting married to Christy for over two years now. His past thoughts echoed in his head, *as soon as I graduate and get something that pays a little better . . . something in my field.* But that day had not yet come. He had applied, for close to two and a half years, to every newspaper, magazine, management, teaching, graphic arts, library, technical writing, marketing, business communications and miscellaneous writing job in the area. Within the last few months, he had branched out to Portland and even Seattle in hopes of drawing from a larger market. *Would it maybe take moving to the larger city to make the connection?* It seemed to Dave that his choices always landed him in the wrong place at the wrong time. Somehow, he was his own worst enemy, but he would have rather written it off to bad luck.

Dave knew of people that he graduated with, with the same degree and lower GPAs, and not even close to earning academic honors, that had already found gainful employment, most of which was in their field. Of course, none of them had any leads for him. Dave had a great resume and a portfolio of videos and written pieces that he had amassed during his college career. This didn't seem to matter.

Was it his age? He had attended a community college in the Bay Area when he was 19, fully believing that he was going somewhere with his life, and although he was extremely intelligent, his lackadaisical effort and average grades began to say otherwise. He dropped out after two years because he wanted to work for awhile and to find himself. *How many 21 year olds say the same thing?* What he found out was that he smoked a lot of pot the first year then drank a lot the second and third years, finally of age, although that never seemed to matter before. He had been barely clinging to any job that he could, just to pay the bills and have party cash. He was living the single life.

Following this three year intermittent bender, he had gotten back into shape and cleaned up his act enough to land a management job. He managed a larger health club for close to six years. The pay was good and the benefits were great; free reign of the facilities and discounts on athletic products and supplements. Actually, he hadn't looked or felt so good since high school, when he thought that he might become the next great catcher or outfielder for the San Francisco Giants. Back then, he could hit as well or better than most and had an arm that could peg a runner stealing second while throwing from his haunches. And, he was fast. Really fast. He led his high school division, and then the region, in stolen bases. This was no small feat for a half time catcher. Of course, this was all before his knees gave out halfway through his Senior year while he was playing varsity football. That stopped the pro recruiters from coming around and effectively ended his baseball career.

For awhile, Dave enjoyed his life as the athletic manager: flirting with the single women who entered to do aerobics classes or tan, working out two or more hours a day, performing personal training to educate people about fitness, dieting and work out schedules, and feeling a great sense of pride in his work. After all, he was helping people achieve their goals of becoming healthy. And, healthy people are happy people, he had often thought. Of course, he looked great.

Then one day, something snapped . . .

What the hell am I doing? My life sucks! It has no meaning. I spend my days telling people how to lift weights and run on a treadmill like a hamster, while they tell me about their problems. I'm a fitness bartender who has to listen to everyone's hang ups about their own personal issues that are always self serving and never scratch the surface of any true form of deeper existence. There's got to be more to life than moving on through the world in a manner that is wrought with superficiality and is filled with the feeding of people's egos and the placating of my brain and body with female eye candy at work and the extremely dim, large busted, attractive women which I hunt down for pleasure, of which there is no shortage of, on Friday and Saturday nights in the bars. Isn't there more? Is this it? IS THIS IT?! Where is the creativity? What is my purpose?! Why am I here? Is this going to be the mark I leave on this world? Where is the lasting relationship? Where's the family? Where is my soul mate? Does she even exist? Does he who dies with the most toys really win? Is the only goal in life to leave a beautiful corpse? Is there someone, that special someone, like what you read about in romance books or see on TV? That one person, where you both grow old together, and know each other's every thought and feeling, and finish each other's sentences, and wash the car together, and sit around and talk about books, or watch movies on a Saturday night after cooking each other a big spaghetti dinner and having a glass or two of good wine, and staying up until the early morning and talking about religion, or philosophy, or love, or even what it means to be a person, all after the kids have gone to bed? Is she going to walk into a fitness meat-market or a bar? Is this the rest of my goddamn my life? Is this the extent of my capabilities and desires? I WANT TO WRITE! I WANT TO RESEARCH! I WANT TO PUBLISH! I will be the first one in my family to finish college! My own words, spoken not too long ago, now almost forgotten, lost in a sea of pointless subsistence and confusion. What am I doing with my life?

So Dave gave his notice, just like that.

Dave moved to Eugene, Oregon, and took the few remaining courses he needed for his AA transfer degree at the community college there. Once that was completed, that first step, he applied to the University of Oregon, he was accepted, and he worked very, very hard. Dave graduated Summa Cum Laude, with honors, and was elected to two national honors societies. He did all of this while working 50 to 60 hours per week, nights and weekends, at the imaging center. He managed to survive on an average of five hours of sleep per night, but in his mind, it was all going to be worth it, someday. His father had always told him that the sacrifice *always* pays off in the end.

Dave's professors doted on his hard work and told him that he was very talented and should have no trouble at all finding well paying and rewarding employment. He had the grades. He had the personality. He had the recommendations. He had the portfolio. He had the attitude. He had the drive. Cut to more than two years after graduation . . .

Dave heard the front door open and he quickly looked at the clock. 1:45pm. He thought, *I guess the referring physician's offices are back from lunch.* Betty was walking around the corner, adjusting her young, chunky but pretty, painted plastic face, coming back from her extended lunch break.

Candy spoke to Dave quietly and quickly, "Believe me Davey, I wouldn't want you to leave. You are really fun to have around here." She smiled but her eyes wandered now to the clock as Betty cleared a few papers from her area and sat down to log onto her terminal. "Dave, Sweetie, you should go to lunch, hun."

He grabbed the completed letters, filed them in a small box marked "to be mailed," logged off of his computer, and walked past Candy, and then Betty, who was now primping her hair in a pink compact mirror.

"See ya Dave" Betty said without looking up from the mirror. He didn't respond, and just kept moving. He turned the corner to head down the long, plainly painted hallway toward his locker in the Men's room. He grabbed his bag lunch and finally hit the time clock to punch out for his half hour of freedom. *Parole?*

He exited into the hallway, through an employee door that was located farther down the same wall as the front door that lead into the reception area. This was the more secret door that the average person didn't know about.

Dave pulled his Ray Ban sunglasses out of his jacket pocket and put them on one handed, carrying his lunch with the other hand. He had ordered the sunglasses special order. They were the Balorama model; the one's that Clint Eastwood had worn in the *Dirty Harry* films. There was something empowering about them to Dave. They were outdated, and he had had them a long time, but he just couldn't seem to part with them. *Sometimes you just can't let go.*

Following the hallway, he stepped across faded, lavender and red paisley printed indoor and outdoor carpet, to the elevators where he pushed the down arrow. It flashed, and then it held a muted green as he waited for the elevator car to reach the third floor, his floor.

Dave glanced at his cheap but stylish Fossil watch and thought, *here's my lunch break just clicking away from me.* He then looked around to see patients and families making their way in and out of the hospital. The third floor not only housed Medical Imaging Center and several ancillary service centers, but on the outside of the building doors it was also the last level of parking. In addition, there was a sky bridge with large glass windows that lead from just past the imaging center, across Parker Avenue, to where most of

Blessed Heart Hospital was located. This floor had the most foot traffic and was well worn to prove it.

The patients moved slowly; the families moved quickly. There were elderly people scooting their walkers and dragging large green oxygen tanks. Other patients were walking toward the outside, wearing blue, white, red or flower printed gowns, to have a cigarette. Others followed in surgical masks and scrubs, lighters and cigarettes in hand.

Something about health care professionals smoking never set right with Dave. Receptionists, that was one thing, but people who actually went to school to study health and medicine? The people who made an informed decision to choose to destroy their own bodies willingly, they were to be the caretakers of others' lives? *How reassuring.*

There was a young, very pregnant woman wearing a long blue oversized t shirt, black stirrup pants and flip-flops (swollen feet), holding her lower back and complaining of pain to a young tall and thin man walking with his arm around her and trying to be as accommodating an one can when his partner is in the last stages of pregnancy.

There were several mother and child or father and child combinations making their way across the sky bridge, carrying candy, flowers or large brightly colored balloons that read "Get Well Soon" or "We Love You." There was one balloon in particular, carried by a large, burley, Biker looking man, that said, "So you're in the hospital . . . eh, it could be the morgue." Dave couldn't imagine who would have had the huevos to give that one, but he thought that it was still pretty damn funny anyway.

There were technologists or surgeons on break, covered head to toe in plain colored scrubs, with pale yellow masks pulled down around their throats and clear looking foot covers over their shoes. Some of them sat and complained about the day, some of them headed toward the lunch room on the other side of the sky bridge and a few of them frantically pulled boxes of Marlboros or Camels and Bic lighters from their pockets as they half walked, half ran past the elevators to the doors leading outside to the uncovered parking area. Rain or shine, an addiction is an addiction. *Maybe everyone has some sort of vice, some sort of escape from reality, even if it is just tar and nicotine. Maybe that keeps us all sane.*

The elevator beeped, the down light returned to its unlit clear phase, and Dave stepped on board with several other people.

As he rode down to the first floor, he could smell the sickness around him. It enveloped and engulfed him. The elevator was hot and humid. He was amidst a swirling sea of strong perfume, body odor, hair spray, bad breath and tobacco. He never got used to taking the elevator and wondered why he hadn't just used the stairs. He thought, *it was just that one time, people can't always be this disgusting.* Then, he'd make the same mistake again, over and over and over.

People coughed. People sniffled. A large lady in a pink flower patterned moo moo dress let loose a big uncovered sneeze that made a few people jump and made her large ankles quiver. It was followed by "God bless you" several times and even a "Gazzunheit." She wiped her nose with her hand and then she wiped her hand on her dress.

The doors opened and Dave pushed his way out, looking down to make sure that his lunch wasn't crushed as the herd evacuated the small elevator car. He walked out of the building and, noticing that the rain from the morning had subsided, he chose to walk across the street to the small benches in the even smaller courtyard next to the parking garage.

He smelled light purple lilac blooms from the trees planted near the medical building. He smelled big pink and red roses. He approached a wooden bench. He breathed in the fresh natural scents slowly as the muted sun peered through the clouds and washed down over his face, giving him a sense of warmth on that early fall afternoon. He had lost the olfactory images of the elevator and was now briefly in his own little world of serenity.

It was after the major lunch rush of workers coming to and from the hospital, like bees to the hive, so the tree blooms and roses were not overpowered by the usual stench of exhaust from the street immediately next to the courtyard. For now, it was a small bit of paradise.

He sat down and opened his lunch bag, pulling out a roast beef and cheddar sandwich. He took a big bite then reached in a pulled out his RC cola, which was wrapped in tin foil. He preferred RC because it had the most sugar out of the big three, Coca Cola, Pepsi and of course, RC Cola. The drink wasn't quite cold, because he forgot to put it in the lounge room refrigerator. He took a sip, swallowed hard and then he said, "not that bad" remembering that the last few times his soda had made it to the fridge, it had been stolen. There's something about work refrigerators that brings out the worst in people. Food and drinks would regularly come up missing. The higher ups had a separate, locked eating room that was more like a fully equipped lounge. They would send out some memo, and the thievery would cease for a little while. But any drinks, especially those with a lot of sugar and caffeine, would fall prey first.

The final item in his bag was a Twinkie. Dave had never quite been able to kick the junk food habit. It had gotten better when he was at the health club and constantly surrounded by several half naked, in-shape people. That was a time was when fitness was his life. Being a gym rat can have its advantages.

But since going back to college, he had gained an increasing appetite for burgers, greasy french fries, pizza and of course, sweets. With a limited budget, the food binges led to other times of Ramen noodles; however, it was never enough to keep him thin. He had gained over twenty five pounds and rarely worked out. Dave had gotten far away from the way that he wanted to present himself; smart and fit. He'd go through a burst for a week or two, but then life would take over and he would succumb to stress by going home and drinking a few cold ones while watching a movie. *Ah, sweet release.*

He finished up lunch, crumpled the bag, tossed it in the shiny metal trash can, and went back in to work. He again used the more secret employee door to enter the imaging center. Dave still had a few minutes to get to his locker and punch in, so he didn't want to run the risk of losing that precious time. He had learned that if you were to come in through the front doors and the receptionists at the desk were busy, you'd be put to work and have to clock in when it got slower. Not exactly legal, but it was a situation easily avoided by using the correct door. Besides, at this job, you learned that the doctors didn't give a shit about anything but themselves and as a subordinate employee you work when they tell you to work, lunch break or not. Doctors usually have a lot of attorney golf buddies, so complaining was pointless, especially to Janet.

The rest of the day went along fairly normally. It wasn't slow, but it wasn't unbearable either. He moved along at a good click, taking people's names, entering their information, pulling their charts and paperwork, taking them to the dressing rooms, and eventually heading them down the hall in the direction of his or her respective examination.

At one time, when he first started working the day shift, there had been a host person to receive the patients from the front desk. The duties of this designated host person were to make sure that each of the patients was changed into the proper exam attire, and cordially walked down to the examination rooms. This extra service actually did help to calm the nerves of patients and allow them a bit of personal service before the sometimes invasive procedures.

It was that little bit of personal service, the little extra effort, that could take the edge off for a patient and make their experience a little more tolerable. These are the things that weren't necessarily measured in a spreadsheet, but still offered a great deal of worth to any sort of business. The official host person would then personally take the patient back to their examining technologist, and along the way try to be as comforting and chatty as he or she could be. This small service on the part of the imaging center and the host person meant a great deal to the patients. But, there hadn't been a host person for several months now. That was another one of Rochelle's brilliant ideas to try and cut corners, and it did save money, so management liked the idea. Now once again, the front desk had picked up even more overflow duties from the other areas. *Couldn't the techs change their own patients since there is no host person? They're just sitting back there waiting, anyway.*

Reception had already inherited more than half of the Medical Records Department's duties when the company went "filmless" and laid off seven full time film file workers. This process was at the request of the film file lead, and of course Rochelle agreed stating that the so called "cross training" for the reception staff helped to promote a greater sense of efficiency and also a sense of job security. That last phrase tasted particularly bitter to anyone who had watched their friends from film file walking out for the last time after losing their job.

At the end of the day, when Dave had finished closing down the reception area in preparation for the night person, he looked around to make sure that he wasn't missing anything. He had locked the front door. In the evenings, the door ran off of a cheap plastic remote control that was held together by Scotch tape and looked like a worn garage door opener from the 1970's. He shut down all but one of the computers and then he picked up any miscellaneous paper coffee cups, pop cans, candy wrappers or newspapers lying around in the lobby. He had drawn the shades on the windows, rearranged the chairs and tables to their original stations, counted out the money in the till and locked up the supply cabinets. The center was now officially ready for the night shift.

Gary, a tall man in his early fifties with a big black and silver peppered moustache and collar length matching hair, walked around the corner to take over for Dave. Gary had been a logger in his younger days, but he had broken his back working green chain and had to take to something a little less physical. When he was offered the late shift, he had told Janet that he actually preferred it because he was a night owl. That might have had something to do with it, but it was much more likely that after his working for twenty plus years in the forested hillsides of Oregon, he had gotten used to dealing with very few people at a time. His interpersonal skills were limited to begin with. He was a nice guy, but he knew there was no way in hell that he could have taken days. He was glad that Dave went to mornings because the night position had opened up for him at the right time.

Gary asked, "Hey, you outta here, buddy?"

"Hell yes!" They both laughed a little.

"Tough day at the ol' corral?"

"Not too awful bad, but it's time to go. Knowadimean?" After a second he said, "I picked up pretty well and the rooms seem to be pretty full so you won't have to do too much stocking."

Gary Replied, "That's good cuz I'm beat. I had a helluva time sleepin' this mornin'. My damn neighbor was out and revving his engine in that old Buick Riviera he's tryin' to fix. I finally had to yell out the window, 'Give it a rest, Pal!'" Gary looked disgusted with the whole ordeal.

"Yeah, I hate it when people are like that. What did the guy do?"

"Oh, his old lady was out there and she turned around and spouted somethin' 'bout it bein' a free country or somethun. I can't just remember it right. She pissed me off, though."

"Yeah?"

Gary's face lightened up. He replied, "yeah. I told 'em both to take it sumwhur else or I was a callin' the manager, 'cuz they ain't supposed to be workin' on cars in the carport anyhow. That shut 'em up, shut 'em up good, it did."

Dave Laughed a little then said, "Well, hopefully tonight it will be pretty easy for you, here at work at least."

Gary sat down to log on to the computer and he looked back over his shoulder at Dave and said, "Great! Although, as I'm sure ya know, the busier ya stay, the less billin' and collectin' calls you gotta to make." He paused for a moment, and then he pulled on the end of his moustache, and continued, "I hate makin' those goddamn calls. If a guy answers, he thinks you're tryin' to pork his old lady. If its a lady, 'specially an old one, ya end up on the phone for a half hour or worse, talkin' 'bout geraniums or something. And everyone's always in the middle of dinner, or puttin' down the kids for bed or sumpum, ya know?"

"Yeah, I hear ya. I've been through all that and I don't miss that part of the night shift."

"It still beats days though, at least in my opinion."

"There are plusses and minuses to everything, I guess," Dave replied.

"Yup, you got it."

The buzzer rang and they both looked up to see a patient standing at the door, waiting to be let in. She pulled on the door and rang the buzzer again. Gary grabbed the remote and pointed it at the door, clicking it repeatedly. He whispered, "They never time it right. Half the time, I gotta to git up and open the damn thing myself." This time, though, the patient understood. She opened the door and walked through, making sure it closed behind her, and then headed for the counter. Dave almost saw the situation as a soft, reminiscing moment as compared to the day shift. But then, he was ready to leave.

"I gotta jet, Chet. See you, tomorrow." Dave grabbed his sunglasses case from the desk and walked around the corner to the hallway.

"Yeah, see ya, Dave."

CHAPTER 5

The champagne had really knocked Kennedy down. He was dead asleep. Only his cat Emily could hear how loud he was snoring. Alcohol did that to him, when he drank a little too much. He'd take in a short breath, followed by a longer chugachugchug exhale, then a long breath, and another chugachugchug.

The moonlight drifted through the open window and reflected off of his face, highlighting the tiny blond, brown, and the few gray hairs in his beard. After a few hours, when most of the champagne had worked its way through his system, his breathing relaxed. He was peacefully enjoying his deep sleep slumber.

While he slept with Emily curled on the blankets at his feet, the wind blew its soft breath through his open bedroom window. The delicate curtains flitted about, back and forth, gently dancing to a beat only they could understand. The moon had moved across the sky and now came in the window much more directly. It hit the face of Kennedy's wind up alarm clock that read 3:37am The moonlight sparkled in the glass of water on the nightstand and lit up nearly the entire room with a sweet and puffy glow.

Emily's ear twitched. She sat up quickly and looked toward the window. She shivered, then she uttered a faint and cautious, "reeooow," but it was not enough to awaken Kennedy. Her fur stood up a little on her back. She looked to Kennedy and then she jumped down from the bed, hardly making a sound, missing the large burgundy, tan and indigo area rug, hitting the hardwood floor. She scampered off down the hall, and then down the stairs to the living room. She hid under the couch. Only her bright green, almond shaped eyes showed, reflecting what little moonlight came in through the sliding glass door that led to the back patio.

Kennedy's bedroom drapes fluttered harder as the wind picked up. It made a distant whistling sound as it wove in between branches of an old weeping willow. The voice of the wind began to change. The whistling was now a sort of static; a ham radio operator searching for a channel. A voice began to come through the dissonance. At first it was garbled and unclear, but then it pushed its way through to a whisper. "Ken-ne-dy . . ." It became louder as the wind got stronger.

His sleep became disturbed. He twisted on the bed, first to the left and then to the right. He began to shiver and unconsciously his arms went up over his naked chest. He laid there in the fetal position shaking, his eyes pinched tight and his lip quivering.

It got unbelievably cold. The bright white light from the moon faded to an ice blue. It got brighter as the voice got closer. The curtains again moved back and forth in one final thrust and then stopped, completely rigid and frozen.

A figure slowly floated in through the window and painted the room with its cold blue eminence. It cast only the blue hue that faded to white as it left the figure. Although its form was there, no details defined it clearly. A young woman's slender and shapely figure could be seen, but it was nearly transparent and her outline was blurry. It glided over and hovered above Kennedy's bed, staring at him curiously in his violent sleep. It called his name again, its breath appearing in a broken, crystalline fog. "Ken-ne-dy . . ."

Kennedy awoke on his back, staring up at and through, the figure. He sunk into his bed, his arms out sideways. His hands gripped the sheets with white knuckles. His muscles tensed. His eyes widened. He tried to scream, but he had no air. His voice was silent.

The outline slowly began to move down, a falling autumn leaf, drifting back and forth like Poe's pendulum.

Kennedy quickly turned away, smacking the nightstand with his hand and knocking the glass of water to the wooden floor with a crash. Shards flew and a pool of water formed around the broken glass. The entity's light reflected from the jagged pieces like crystal blue mosaic.

The figure suddenly stopped and its eyes widened and brightened. It quickly turned and glanced at the small pool of water. It appeared to be startled.

Kennedy could sense a shift in the cold that he felt. The figure swung its arms in front of it, quickly blocking its face. It turned toward the window and became a streak that headed out with such a force that it nearly lifted Kennedy off of the bed.

Kennedy jumped up, careful to avoid the broken glass, and ran to the window. He leaned out and saw the last glimpse of the blue light fading to white as it ducked over a hill, the vapor trail shimmering tiny stars and then fading quickly in the distance. For the moment, Kennedy was alone again. The room grew dark. The moon slowly, slowly reappeared. The temperature returned to normal.

The next few days, all things considered, were fairly normal for Kennedy with the exception that now he was going into the University of Oregon workplace as a fully credentialed professor. That change felt really good. He had convinced himself that the previous events were based on his being exhausted and nervous about his upcoming year of teaching. He had read somewhere that the power of the mind was incredible enough to make anything seem like it was actually happening. It was just a matter of choosing how to perceive it. He heard that once a guy had lifted the front end of a car to save his girlfriend who was trapped beneath it. The guy could do it because his mind told him that it was possible; he had to believe it to allow it to happen. He thought, *what is this ghost stuff all about anyway?*

The sun shone brightly that day in Eugene in middle September, and the temperature was still fairly warm, nearly sixty degrees at 7:30am. Several hundred students were mulling about the campus. The new Freshmen and Junior Transfers were nervously seeking their classes and the returning students were sipping lattes on the old stone steps, or grabbing a veggie bagel sandwich with cream cheese and sprouts, before heading to their first class.

Kennedy smiled when he pulled into his newly assigned parking space. It had the bright yellow and green sign with a large "O" that read "Reserved for Dr. Kennedy Jones. Violators will be towed." This was a bright addition to his teaching life. Having to fight for parking at a major university amongst all the other faculty, students, staff and visitors was now a thing of the past. He had figured that just having a space so close to his class could save him 20 minutes or more in the mornings. Things were really coming together for him.

Kennedy did not have a class until 9:00am, so he thought he would go to his office and get prepared. Even after teaching several courses, over several years, the first day was always a little difficult. There was always that performance anxiety that comes with any teaching job; it is just part of the deal. Learning the names of the new students, figuring out who has what kind of personality and work ethic, learning who is too shy to ever say a word, but will do every assignment asked of him or her, learning who is going to try and continue to be the high school class clown, learning which pretty and smart girl with an overbearing type 'A' personality, who is studying to be a nurse, is going to bitch the entire time because she is *required* to take his *pointless* literature class, learning who is the jock that thinks playing football equates to an automatic passing grade, learning who is the previous high school head cheerleader who has gained fifteen pounds and is now completely displaced and hasn't found a way to correct for years of being adorned and having perfected a status based personality, learning which students are the writers and artists living on the fringe part of society, and which students are really spoiled rotten and rich, but are merely trying to pose as such, and finally learning which students might, just might, actually be taking the class because they have an interest in the material.

There are always so many variables. Each class always has its own personality and it helps to dictate how the term goes. Luckily for Kennedy, this wasn't a high school class and many of the students were in his classes because they wanted to be exposed to the material, or just wanted to take a class from him. Quite often for Kennedy, his reputation for being fair, funny, and a great instructor preceded him.

He walked up to the solid wood door of his office, noticing that his name plaque was not on it yet. *I'll need to make a call about that.* This office was new to him as well. He had previously shared a bullpen office with the graduate student teachers and two other assistant professors from the Foreign Language department, which was housed in the same building as English.

There was a dark wooden desk against the back wall, near a small window. On it, there was a computer monitor, a keyboard, a place for pens and pencils, and an 'in' and 'out' box. There were empty bookshelves behind him that he would soon fill with his numerous volumes of literature and research books, including the ones that he had written himself. Since he had taken his position at the U of O, these books sat in his garage packed away neatly and sealed in air-tight plastic bins. In his classroom, he kept a few books for reference, but the bulk of his collection was packed away. With an office, although it was not large, he now had the room to display more of his written treasures.

Kennedy walked over to the desk, sat down his briefcase and pulled open the window blinds. He slid up the window, taking in the fresh scent of the ancient pine tree just outside. Although the tree had to be more than one hundred years old, the scent was very familiar to him. He sat down in the lightly worn black leather chair and closed his eyes. Content and relaxed, he was lost for a moment in the joyful accomplishment that his life had finally become.

Even with all of the grandeur that accompanied being a full fledged professor, with full tenure, there was still the damn grading. This was perhaps his least favorite part of the job and always had been. He realized that assessment was important, in order to show people where they were and how well they were doing, but that did not make the grading any easier. Some professors pawned off their grading on all of the too eager to please graduate assistants, and there was something to be said for that. But this did not work for

Kennedy. Unfortunately, he cared too much to make sure that the students were actually understanding the material, so he could not farm out his grading. Soon, he would be 'up to his ass in alligators,' as his father used to say, with both creative and analytical pieces of writing, all in need of review and grading. Some of which would be interesting, from those students who used their minds for something other than preparing for the ultimate servicing of the machine (thank you Ken Kesey for your 'Cuckoo's Nest,') but others, the real dread of the grading, would be from those students who took his courses as requirements and only did the bare minimum to get by, no matter what they were capable of doing. That was the frustrating part. To read 50 to 100 papers, all regurgitating the same exact information that he spoke about in class, with no original analysis and no new insights. It was like he was rereading his lesson plans. Swallow, chew, spit out and repeat until graduation; then, do the same thing in the workplace. Many of the modern students lived by the proverbial 'keep your mouth shut and good things are bound to happen.'

It was hard for Kennedy to know that many of the students he had in class would never again think critically or analytically about anything that wasn't earning them money, especially in the realms literature or film. Nope, they would be out in their careers trying to exploit some resource for their own gain, often at the expense of many others. *But, hey, that is Capitalistic America, right? Land of the free, home of the one who has the most stuff? Maybe they're right, and the joke is on me?* Kennedy knew, deep down, that many of those people would never be happy or satisfied, no matter how much money they obtained. But when you had gone through living on Top Ramen every meal for an extended period of time, then you started to understand their shallowness.

Kennedy knew that his job wasn't to save the world. Not even close. His job was to try and enlighten when he could and to teach literature to those willing to, or needing to take his class. And all in all, it was a great profession to be in, and a great job to have.

He walked into his classroom at 8:45am. There were a few students in the halls, probably a few of them would be in his class, but they enjoyed their last few minutes before they had to go in.

Kennedy's first class was an introductory literature class and many of the students only took it for the required Language Arts credits. As such, there was not the enthusiasm of his more advanced classes. Nonetheless, he enjoyed these students as well, feeling that he might open a few of their minds up to something besides Economics, Finance, Calculus or Applied Life Sciences. A few of them would become his students later in their college careers, but most would do the work for the term and then move on linearly with taking only the classes in their chosen fields, avoiding the freaks in the English and Art Halls at all costs.

When the bell rang at 9:00am, Kennedy was standing at the white board. He had already written his name, email address, the phone number to his office, the class period, name of the course, course section number, and his office hours, Tuesdays and Thursdays from 3:00pm to 4:30pm. The students were copying this information down into their notebooks as he began with his catch phrase for the introduction classes, "My Friends, welcome to Fantasy Island."

CHAPTER 6

Dave's small apartment looked as it usually did. It was clean, not unpleasant to be in, and far from being a total hole in the wall. At times it was almost quaint, kind of like the partly dilapidated but warm big city apartments found in a Kerouac novel. But usually, unless Christy was stopping by, it had some sense of sloppiness to it. There were a few articles of clothing scattered on the floor: white socks, navy blue plaid cotton boxer shorts and a plain black t shirt. The plastic blinds needed dusting, the shower needed a light scrubbing, the trash needed taking out and the floors needed a good vacuuming.

His studio apartment was one large room and a bathroom, with a somewhat separated kitchen area that housed an older, olive green refrigerator and a matching stove. The counters were a rust color that matched the pseudo shag carpet. The stainless steel sink was newer, clean, and there were no dishes in the green rubber textured drying rack. Dave knew it was not the greatest place, but it was safe enough, fit into his budget and he could call it home. His Volkswagen was parked between two faded white lines outside the living room window, only separated from the apartment wall by a small cracked cement walkway, much like at an old motel. In fact, he had been told that the apartment building had previously been a motel of sorts until the early 1970s, when it was remodeled and the rooms were made into small apartment units.

Dave had lived there almost six years, since the summer before starting at the university. His rent had not been raised during that time. He was located near the campus, which had been handy on those occasional early school days that followed 75 cent draft Tuesday at Doc's Pad, a local bar and pool hall. Even waking up late, he seemed to get to class just in the nick of time. However, his grades did not suffer. He was a hard worker who believed in the 'work hard, play hard' motto. He maintained a high GPA, especially for working full time. But, his best work was usually at the last minute, at three in the morning. He worked best when under a great deal of pressure; that is when things clicked best for him and he became the most motivated.

The electric buzz saw of his alarm pulled him from sleep. He sat straight up, disoriented, and slammed the top of the imitation wood grain clock. The red led lights dimmed for a second, then returned. 9:00am. "Shit!"

He jumped out of bed and went to the only closet, wondering just how many times he had hit the snooze bar in his sleep. He grabbed a blue *Medical Imaging Center* shirt and pair of black slacks. The company shirts could be different colors, but the black slacks were mandatory. However, if you wanted more than the two shirts you were issued, you had to pay for them yourself.

Dave quickly threw on his clothes and looked around the room. There on the headboard, that's what he wanted . . . *Camel Lights*. He pulled one from the box, removed the match book that he had stuck into the cellophane, and lit the end. He took a deep drag, held it for a second, and then exhaled, coughing a little afterwards.

He shoved the smoke in his mouth, put on his black Sketcher's shoes and went over to the kitchen. He grabbed the clear glass knob of the painted white cupboard, reached in, and pulled out a small box. He opened it, removed two cherry flavored Pop Tarts and shoved them into the toaster. Next, he pulled a plastic cup from the cupboard, opened the refrigerator and poured himself a cup of orange juice. *No time for coffee . . . have to grab that at work*. When the pastries jumped up from the chrome toaster, he snubbed out his cigarette in a small round porcelain ashtray that read, "Harrah's Reno" on it. He downed his juice, grabbed his breakfast and headed out the front door for work.

Upon arriving, he speed walked down the hallway toward the time clock and punched in one minute late. *I'd have been on time if it wasn't for Dianna's big administrative ass taking forever in front of me.* Then he thought, *Maybe there's something to this showing up to work 15 minutes before the start of your shift? Yeah, right.*

The patient flow was steady and he had gotten into his rhythm. Call a name, check their information, pull the paperwork and send them to their room. *One, two, three, four . . . get 'em in and out the door.*

Betty was relaying information to people in her partially hydrogenated way, smiling way too large and forcing her canned office laugh whenever possible. Dana was staring at her computer screen, pretending to be busy, hoping that nobody would catch her spacing off; silently counting the ticks of the clock until she could feasibly head out the door for another smoke break. Such was the pattern of the work day.

Dave smoked regularly, but did not let anyone at work know. Well, except for Gary. If someone saw Dave out on a weekend at one of the local haunts and he had a cigarette in his mouth, he gave them the, "yeah, only when I'm drinking" routine. Powerful breath mints and a good dowse of "Eternity" cologne had seemed to keep everyone from questioning him. He could always control the habit when he wanted to and he didn't even feel the urge for nicotine the whole work day; not even after lunch when most smokers crumble. But when he was on his own time, he chose to ignore what he knew were the right things to do, especially when it concerned making the right choices regarding his own life.

Candy had the day off to go shopping with her eldest daughter. They'd hit Wal-Mart first and then head for the mall if they didn't find the special deal that they were seeking. The item was not so much as important as the fact of getting it at an incredibly discounted price. Neither of them was ever able to earn much more than a basic subsistence of salary. They viewed their victories at the mega sales as would an ancient Cherokee Brave who took a fresh scalp. In both cases, they were getting even with the society that had suppressed them in one way or another.

When it had slowed down, Dave turned to Dana and said, "Hey, I'm taking ten."

She looked up from her expressionless stare, a little shocked, and said, "Uh. Okay, um . . . see you in a few." She snarled slightly because now she would have to take the next patient that came through the door. Betty could put up a good office demeanor, too much so, but she too was frustrated with Dana's lethargic behavior and would not let her skate on the duties. That was one of the reasons that Rochelle doted on Betty so much; they were medical office twins that were separated by only 20 years or so. But, Betty did have a good work ethic and she got things done.

A patient walked in just as Dave had slipped around the hallway entrance. Betty said, "She can help you right here" and guided the elderly couple toward Dana. The two moved very slowly, he dragging behind him an I.V. tube hanging on a tall metal support rod with wheels.

Dana knew that this would take her awhile and more than likely she would have to spend several minutes looking up insurance numbers. The elderly made it a habit of forgetting paperwork, insurance cards, forms and anything else that might make a medical receptionist's job a little easier. She sighed and then said, "Can I help you two?"

Dave walked quickly, passing a few very old "Saturday Evening Post" covers (original ones) that were framed and hung sporadically throughout the hall. The imaging center physicians had expensive tastes, although none of them had ever paid particular attention to any one of the framed covers.

Dave hurried past the time clock and into the employee lounge. It wasn't as nice as the Radiologist's lounge, but it did suffice. Theirs had cable television, a stove, a double fridge, a sink, a shower and a few plush couches. It even had a separate thermostat, to make sure that everything was just perfect in their small sanctuary away from home.

At least in the regular employee lounge, there was a fridge, microwave and what Dave had come in for, a phone that was not in the middle of the reception area. Dave hadn't gotten into the whole cell phone revolution. It seemed silly to pay for two phone bills, especially on his limited income. Besides, there was all that talk about how they caused cancer and he figured that it was bad enough to have to work at an office attached to the hospital, he didn't want to have to come in there as a patient. He'd seen the doctors there pretty close up and although some of them really were miracle workers of sorts, Dave had decided that the public really was better off not knowing what goes on behind the big closed glass doors.

"Sweet. Empty." He dialed the number, pulled out the red chair and sat down. It was uncomfortable, having a chrome metal frame and a one piece plastic shell. It was as if the managers didn't want anyone to be too relaxed for too long. Or maybe the chairs were just cheap. Either way, they were nowhere near the recliners and fancy table chairs to be found next door in the (locked) Radiologist's Lounge.

The phone made a crackly ring in his ear. He could smell the leftover scent of Ravioli and popcorn, fighting for dominance. He heard a female voice pick up, "hello?" It was Christy.

"Hey, girl! Thought you might be at work already."

"No, there's a student orientation for the first half of the day, then I'm in at noon. Are you on break?" She sounded cheerful and glad to hear from him.

"Yeah. I'm wondering what you're doing later tonight? Are you going to be around?" He paused, "It's Friiiiiii-daaaaay!" He sounded a bit like a Frat Boy who had just turned 21.

"Dave, of course I'll be around." She started to sound a little miffed by the question. "You know, if we *lived* together, like *most people* who are engaged, you wouldn't have to ask me what I'm doing later. You could just come home and see for yourself. I might not even be wearing any clothes." Even with the last light hearted comment, she was still squeaking her point across more blatantly than normal.

Dave and Christy had been engaged for four months now, but had not moved in together because of his financial concerns. It had nothing to do with the whole 'not living together until married' thing. She didn't make much more money than him, but she had achieved her goal to become an elementary school teacher and she was good at it. No, she was *great* at it. She loved it and everyone loved her. Dave had always envied the ease with which she had graduated, found a job in her field and settled into a happy little routine. Her life seemed to be like that, though. She enjoyed the moment and didn't worry so much about the small stuff. Life moved freely through her and she let it. Dave was too proud and stubborn to move in with her until he could pay at least half of the bills; however, even he was secretly wearing thin on this entire situation.

"Honey, we've been over this. It's cheaper for me to stay at my place than to pay half of your rent." He paused, and then continued, "And I know how much you *love* the idea of living at my place." This was very sarcastic as Christy and her cat could hardly fit into his place, let alone all of her clothes and furniture.

"Dave, it doesn't have to be fifty percent each right now. You know, what's mine is mine and what's yours is mine?" She chuckled, and then continued. "I know that you're looking for something better than what you have for a job. And, aren't you even thinking about the PhD program at the university? You know how they love you at that school. I think that might be a good route for you. For us."

It was true about Dave. His professors had always admired his work, so much so that he'd even gotten one of his pieces published in a national review through the help of one of his professors. The PhD program would be a shoe in.

Dave rolled his eyes, but kept his composure. "I just need to find something better than the imaging center, something that pays better. When there's more money . . ." He caught himself. "Okay, I'll tell you what. Let's talk about it over dinner. I'll pick you up at, say 6:30 tonight? We'll get pizza or something. Deal?" He looked at the round black and white plastic clock on the wall. Its clear face had a small crack. His last minute of break was quickly ticking away.

"Sure, Dave. But let's make it 7:00pm, I have to grade some papers and don't want to be up all night doing it."

"I wouldn't mind being up all night *doing it*." He laughed a little too loud, intentionally.

"Play your cards right big boy and we'll see what happens."

"Yeah?"

"Yeah." Her tone had lightened substantially. He envisioned her sitting there thinking, *at least he was going to talk about it*. In his mind, Dave had bought himself some more time and he had kept Christy from being upset. *Cool.*

"Love you."

"Love you, too. See you at seven." He hung up the scratched black handle in the equally as worn holder on the wall, trying to unwind the knotted phone cord before doing so.

When he returned to the desk area, Dana was already grabbing her purse to leave and speaking very quickly. "I gotta run across to the, uh, hospital to give them this prescription. Be right back." And she was gone.

Dave sat down, looked at Betty who just shrugged her shoulders, and he smiled back at her. They each knew what the other was thinking. Betty even said, "That looked more like a CT questionnaire than a prescription in her hand."

The day went by steadily, but quickly. The television made its way through the game shows and on in to the soap operas. "The Bold and the Beautiful" was on when Dave noticed that it was nearing his lunch time. Since the foot traffic of the office had slowed a little, he thought it best he make a break for it.

His lunch was spent just across the hall from the imaging center's employee door. The early autumn rains had begun and the temperature outside had dropped accordingly. Dave sat in a plain colored, cushy seat near a window at the entrance to the sky bridge. He rarely liked to sit there because everyone going to or coming from the hospital had to stop and give whoever sat there a good 'once over' glance. It never meant anything, but it was annoying. *Look at the imaging counter jockey eating his greasy burger . . . working in a woman's position . . . get a real job there Buddy!* Today, he bought a cheap lunch because he had left his apartment too quickly to make something, and the pop tars had worn off hours ago.

Dave took a bite and then stared out to the hospital. The water was falling hard enough that large drops and streaks of drizzle ran down the outside of the glass and gave a surreal blur to the building across the street.

As he chewed, he saw the outlines of nurses shifting pillows behind patient's necks. He saw doctors reading charts and medical personnel in scrub clothing walking by windows, holding lattes and clipboards, and speaking to each other with large smiles on their faces. He set down the burger on its wrapper, on top of a short wooden table in front of him. He grabbed his flat, syrupy soda and slurped a big gulp through the straw.

He thought, *how do they do it? How do they go to work everyday and slave away for a company that doesn't care? Most of them seem to be happy. Well, okay, the doctors . . . I understand. Give me three quarters of a million dollars a year and I'd be pretty friggin' chipper too. But the techs and the support staff . . . they don't make anywhere near that much; more than me . . . but that's not saying too much . . . is it? Are they all really that lame? Or, am I just not getting what its all about?*

No! That's bullshit! Some day, I'll be out of this godforsaken place for good.

That idea of returning to school for the PhD program was sounding better all the time. He knew that he wasn't the type to go to tech school or any other vocation for that matter. His father, a self taught computer programmer and network specialist, wanted him to follow in his footsteps. He'd always say, "Things are different nowadays. You need that CS or CIS or MIS degree. I was lucky that I got into it when I did." Of course, that was after many years of either driving for or managing trucking companies.

His father, who was generally a workaholic, had always complained about the long hours and hard work of when he was working for those transportation companies. The funny thing about it was that it never got any better or easier when he had gotten into computers. Every time Dave spoke with his father, there was some major computer crisis going on that took him long hours into the night to fix, severely decreasing his hourly wage. Sure, maybe he wasn't breaking his back loading and unloading trucks, or going half crazy trying to rescue a load of razor blades from a truck that just flipped on the freeway in Arizona, but he seemed to be just as stressed, and when the business got slower and the money got tighter, even more so.

Dave's father was one of the true 24/7 workers, to the point that if he went to a family member's house and had to stand around idle for too long, he would get out their vacuum, or begin trying to repair something. It might seem a bit obsessive and compulsive, and it probably was, but Dave's father couldn't help it. Besides keeping himself busy, he was actually trying to help. He was like so many men of his era, *always* needing to be doing something productive. Stagnation was not an option and it made him crazy. Just relaxing for the pure enjoyment of it was not something that was in his vocabulary.

Dave's first two semesters in college were actually spent studying in a computer science major. It bored the shit out of him and he really didn't see the point of doing all that math work. Dave thought of himself as more of a PBS mathematician and scientist. He understood all of the concepts, but didn't have the patients for all of the associated number crunching work. *Can't computers already do all of these stupid rudimentary calculations? What the hell did Isaac Newton and Albert Einstein and even M.C. Escher do all their work for in the first place if we just have to repeat it? Seems like a waste of time.*

About the only thing that was directly passed down from his father, other than some of his good looks, was his smoking habit. Even with a diagnosis of a precancerous larynx, his father, Richard (Rick), wouldn't give it up. "When I go, I'll go. I'm going to live my damn life the way I feel . . . full of smoke if I choose it, having a drink when I want it. And, eating whatever the hell I goddamn please!" His father lived on a steady diet of hamburgers and whole milk, with the occasional chicken fried steak and gravy thrown in for good measure. Vegetable intake mainly consisted of lettuce consumed on the bun of a Jack in the Box 'Jumbo Jack.'

It was a regular thing for his father to make fun of vegetarians and the Eugene area in general. He'd say, "those damn tree huggin', vedgy-eatin' bleeding heart Liberals! They're what's wrong with this country. They don't understand that money makes the world go 'round and that the resources are what gives us the money. And all those social welfare programs, what a bunch of crap! And they don't have any family values or morals, passin' out condoms to kindergarteners." He would continue, "Yeah, a Liberal is just a Conservative who hasn't been mugged yet." And although he had close to an opposite political viewpoint, in some respects, Dave thought that his father was sometimes right.

Dave knew that Rick spoke for what a good percentage of people in America believed, but Eugene and Oregon in general were a little bit different. The people there did lean toward the liberal side and believed in saving the environment, guaranteeing animal rights and supporting social assistance programs. Although Dave was not as extreme as many in the area and he could understand all of the points that his father brought up as being at least in part valid, he still leaned more toward the 'left of center.'

At least his father's drinking had come under control. When he was very young, while his parents were still married, he hated to see his father come home, wake up the family at four in the morning, back from a week on a long haul truck route, drunk, stinking of smoke and ready to fight anyone in his way. Many nights, he had already been in to a fight earlier that evening. Dave's mother had ended up in the hospital with a split lip and a concussion one night when Dave was seven; that was one of the final things that lead to his parent's divorce.

Dave's father moved to Washington State and at that time began to get involved with computers. He read books and studied electronics until he could begin his own repair shop out of his house. Eventually, his knowledge got him a job with an up and coming Seattle outfit, Compusoft, where he worked for several years, until partly retiring and opening another home based business.

Rick *had* to work. He had enough money to retire, easily, but the idle time would have driven him mad. Even when they were just talking or having a slower paced get together, Rick had to always be fidgeting with something. His mind was always active.

Following the divorce, Dave's mother, Janey, worked as a waitress; usually double shifts. She raised Dave in Northern California until after he graduated high school. Then, she moved to Eugene, Oregon after Dave had entered the local California Community College and found his own apartment. Janey was finally able to buy a small two bedroom house in a decent part of town. It was quaint and it was just enough for her.

Dave and his mom had always lived in apartments since the divorce. He had never gone without, but had never had some of the other things his friends had either. He saw his father once or twice a year, sometimes only once in every two years. He often thought that he was glad that he didn't have any other siblings, especially a sister. It was hard enough for him, but he had thought that a young girl would have been traumatized much more severely than he was at the tragedies he had faced in his youth.

Although he never felt particularly threatened, the lower rent area that he had grown up in was not the best. Dave regularly would see people buying and selling drugs, trying to look as inconspicuous as possible. There were prostitutes near the 7-11 store that was maybe five blocks from his house. Of course, he only saw them after dark, usually when he was riding his bicycle home from baseball or football practice. They would cat call to him and laugh as he rode by and tried to ignore them.

The sides of his apartment building that he lived in while growing up would end up with graffiti spray painted on them, usually the current tag of whoever was in power at that time. However, even with all of that negativity influencing his childhood, he was never accosted and he still kept a positive attitude about school, sports and people in general. That doesn't mean that it was easy and he was often jealous, especially when he got older, of those naïve kids who grew up in the all white neighborhoods and had everything that they wanted handed to them without ever having to work for any of it, or even understanding what they had.

Even though Janey did everything that she could, Dave sometimes felt like he had been robbed of his childhood innocence way too early. Having to assume the role of the 'man of the house' at seven, with no father figure at home to raise or mentor him, left a mark that lasts a lifetime. But, Dave had always respected his mother for everything she did for him and he knew that she did everything she could to make his life better. He also knew that despite everything, his mother and father were much better off apart than they ever were together.

Dave had grown tough and had put it all behind him. He and his father had even come to positive terms in recent years. His father had apologized to both Dave and Janey, numerous times for his previous behavior. Dave figured that his mother and father were just too young when they got married; they had both said as much. Dave had written the whole thing off to life lessons learned. At least he had been able to finally let the bitterness pass and begin to try and understand and try to build a relationship with his father again.

His mother, who had passed away of cancer when Dave was twenty two, had never graduated high school because of giving birth to him when she was fifteen. His father was only seventeen. She was so proud to see David go back to college, especially to attend a prestigious, PAC 10 university. To her, that gave it all the more distinction. She had often told him that she had seen herself becoming a lawyer when she was younger, before her life choices had nixed that plan.

Although she never got to see Dave walk across that stage with his black robe, matching hat, and gold and emerald honors tassels rocking back and forth with each step on that sunny day in June, she filled his mind and heart that day.

He did it as much for her as for his own benefit. Rick was unable to attend the graduation and had been away at a programming seminar in Minneapolis. Dave remembered his father's voice on the phone saying, "Does your graduation have to be on that day? I can't change the day that they teach the training, ya know. Well, at least you got the degree, that is all that really matters. I am proud of you for that." Dave's father had shown up for a few days the following weekend, and they did have a bit of a belated celebration at that time. Albeit late, it was a good time for them both.

Dave was trying to block out the Muzak playing in the background of the imaging center office. He watched another elderly patient trudge slowly across the floor, the back of her faded white, flower printed gown almost flopping open with every step, nearly revealing the aged, overweight, dehydrated, wrinkled and naked body beneath. He thought, *how inhumane to have to go through this humiliation just for a cigarette*, as he finished off his burger and grabbed a Snickers from his jacket pocket.

What the hell am I suppose to be learning? That I can just eddy around here in stale water amongst the other stagnated creatures? He stopped, tore open the Snickers and took a big bite. As he chewed, his thoughts continued. *Does it even really matter? I followed all the proper channels . . . I went to school . . . I did what I was supposed to do. I even put myself in serious debt with student loans to do it! Um, hello?! Where's the damn 'ca-ching' at the end of the rainbow?!*

He stood up, frustrated, and walked back through the employee door, trying to calm himself down and sweeten his bitterness so that it didn't lurch forth and project itself onto the people he was to be assisting. It wasn't much of a job, but, he *was* at work. Those people had enough crap going on, they didn't need his too. He finished out his day, the same as usual.

Dave's Volkswagen rolled up in front of Christy's two story townhouse just after 7:00pm. The light green paint on the building and the darker green on the trim were both fresh, done within the last month and the hedges were trimmed square. Each building had a well manicured fir tree in the front yard. Christy had planted a few rows of deep navy blue, lemon yellow and pure white pansies on either side of the cleanly swept, cobblestone walkway. They had fully blossomed, but would fade and die by the end of fall, in a few short months. She had vowed to renew them every spring and even though she knew the flowers were to die, she enjoyed the feeling that they gave her while they were there. Pansies were nice in that they were always easy to bring back. They were different blossoms, but the same plant. She liked that idea and she found it very spiritual.

Christy lived off of the main streets and away from the lower rent districts that had become Dave's forte. He had never had any problems; no robberies, no muggings, no crack dealers outside and no pimps beating their wig wearing whores in the next apartment over. On the contrary, his inexpensive apartments usually sided with elderly people on fixed incomes; their pale grey and blue hair reflecting bright as they would leave tuna out for cats that they didn't own and spend money they didn't have on feeding the ducks a loaf or two of dried bread every Sunday afternoon at the local man made pond. Their lives were simple.

Christy saw Dave pull up through her living room window. The blinds closed and then she came out of the door and locked it behind her. She wore baggy gauze style pants and a snuggly fitting tank top with an open sheer white blouse over it. As she walked to the car, the light evening breeze tossed her almost waist length blond hair to and fro. The setting sun shimmered its last rays off of her soft, naturally tanned skin, moving gently from her hair to her chin, pausing only briefly along the way for a glimpse into her bright green eyes. She got into his car, she liked the classic Volkswagen bugs for some strange reason, and then they headed out for pizza.

About half way there, they decided that Chinese food sounded better. There was a great vegetarian place that Christy loved to take him to. He always put up a fight, but ended up enjoying anything they ordered. They parked across the street and went into The Lotus Garden.

Once inside, there were several intricate Pagodas shining dim yellow light. Combined with the faint scent of incense, it gave the small restaurant a peaceful, subdued feel to it. The walls held a few pictures of Chinese waterfalls and a man pulling a plow behind an ox, through a large, grassy field. He was working the land like the traditional workers, with his hands. Christy and Dave sat across from each other in one of four high back, black leather booths. The rectangular table had a silver edge to it and the table ran between them from the wall to the end of the seats.

After their waiter brought them their waters and they ordered some sort of fake meat sweet and sour pork, Christy reached out and grabbed up Dave's hands into hers. They would take a moment to stare into each other's eyes and smile, just for being together. It was some little ritual that they had begun on their first date. They had been doing it for a few years now, but it seemed like a lot longer and felt a lot stronger than that.

When they had met, something had just clicked. They were in college, at about the same class level. Juniors. Life was always bright and full of aspirations; they were to have the prefect future once their learning was done. *Isn't that how it's supposed to be?*

Since then, Christy had started her career teaching and Dave was still looking for something better than the imaging center could provide him. Christy thought nothing of Dave's situation, other than what he made of it. He would pass up invitations to some of her more formal evening academic functions, feeling that he'd have to hang himself if anyone with a real job ever found out what he did for a living, and with a Bachelor's degree to boot.

But, if he stayed at the imaging center forever, she wouldn't care. Dave could pump gas or shovel horse droppings as long as he was content and happy with his life. Christy loved him for him, when he allowed himself to be 'him.' Dave was at his best when he was playing guitar, drawing, making short films and most of all writing, writing, writing. Writing had been his thing, since he was a 6th Grader writing mysteries at a high school level. Lately, more often than not, Dave just complained and felt sorry for himself. He was either depressed or pissed off. The once plentiful happy times were becoming fewer and much further in between.

Dave had always felt secretly jealous of Christy's success in adapting to post graduation life. He tried not to show it and kept it hidden quite well, or so he thought, but she could always sense the distance. She would ask herself, *is this why he won't move in with me? Does he need to get it together before he feels that he is ready to share his life completely with someone else? Or, is it the self constructed inadequacies that are keeping him stalled where he is in life?*

Christy asked, "So, how was the rest of your day at Nuke City?" He laughed softly. It was always nice to hear Christy's lighthearted view on things. And, with all of the reports of the damage that too many rads could do to someone, she had a good point in her commentary.

"You know . . . same ol', same ol'. Another day, another 500 patients." He pulled his hands back a little and then reached for his glass of ice water. Suddenly he felt warm, like he was caught surprisingly wearing a jacket when the sun's mid day heat moved out from behind a thick cloud. He gulped his water and then he continued, "How 'bout you?"

"Are you okay, Dave? You seem, preoccupied or something." She now reached for her water and took a drink as well. The last thing she wanted was to put him off, to get him into a mood where he wouldn't open up at all. He could be so close at times and then flee for a much colder and more isolated place. His body would be there, but his mind and soul were far, far away. She would sense her voice echoing back distantly, just bouncing between the high reaching sharp peaks and valleys of glaciers.

"No, I'm good. I'm . . ." He stopped and thought for a second, remembering looking across the sky bridge to the hospital: *all the little hamsters scurrying about pointlessly in their life sized Habitrail*. His mood shifted. "Actually, I'm thinking about pursuing the PhD." Her eyes looked somewhat like a bug might just before hitting the windshield of an oncoming automobile, but, much prettier, of course. "Christy? Are You Okay? Do you need to lie down?" He said this with humor behind it and of course she laughed.

"Yes, I'm fine. You just caught me off guard. I wasn't expecting anything other than . . ."

"Other than what?" He was curious, but not accusatory.

Her lips formed a Mona Lisa smile and the room seemed to brighten just for that second. "Um, Why now?"

He hadn't expected that response from her, "Look, if you think it's a bad idea, then . . ."

She grabbed his hands again, "Of course I think it's a good idea, *if* it's what *you* want. I just want you to be happy. I want *us* to be happy. I know that you're not happy wasting away with people who want to work reception the rest of their lives. You have so much more to offer. And, the PhD program seems like an option that would break this funk you've been in."

Funk? What does she mean? I've never really complained to her, other than joking about work. Nothing serious. It was hard for him to hear this from such a positive person. He often thought that if he were a homeless man lying in the gutter and she smiled once at him in the right way, he could go on living without food forever. But, he rarely let her know that, though. After stifling his quick tempered first reaction, he answered, "I am going to check into it." Then it slipped,

"If life doesn't kick me in the face again." *Shit! Did I just say that? Maybe I haven't been as careful as I thought.*

Christy dropped his hands just as the smell of steamed rice, spicy hot mustard and jasmine tea became intense. Her smile puckered to unripe lemons. Serious. The waiter, not noticing anything about their mood or change of mood, *serve 'em up, move 'em out*, set the food in front of them, asked if they needed anything else, wished them a happy meal and walked back towards the kitchen.

"David, Stop feeling sorry for yourself." Her tone had become aggressive, but remained soft. She called him David, very formal. "Just do *something*. You've been staying with a job you hate for over two years now. Don't ignore where you are in search of where you'll be; the future comes soon enough." She saw his eyes close slightly, like he was measuring her up for his retort. She backed off. "You don't want to be stuck in this circle of redundancy do you?"

This time his eyes were the bugs' eyes, but he didn't react with his normal daggers of icy silence. He was actually curious. *She was never like this, so curt. And what did she mean by 'cycle of redundancy?' Have I done this before? Could it get worse? Are these just the same old footsteps again that I always walk through?*

"Whoa, okay. I'll give you the feeling sorry for myself. I hate my situation right now." Thinking quickly, ". . . Uh, Shit, um." He composed himself. "I mean except for you being in my life and the prospect of us being together forever." He thought, *for—ev—er.*

The food was getting cold. It didn't matter. Christy was now sounding slightly concerned; not her chipper self of an hour ago, but more subdued than a minute ago. "I know that you've been totally hatin' it, especially lately." She glanced at the food quickly, then back to him. She spoke, thinking it best to drop it for the time being. He was thinking about change, and that was good. Enough for now. "The food's gonna need reheating if we take any longer." She smiled and reached for the large serving spoon.

He softly, but quickly grabbed her hand, startling her. He became more serious. "Not just yet."

She released the oversized spoon and looked into his eyes. "Yes, Dave."

He sat back and carefully crafted the presentation of his words. "Christy, what did you mean by going through things again, or however you put it?"

It took her a second. She hadn't even really realized that she had said it. She was expecting more about the PhD, or moving in together, or anything really, besides what he had said. "Um, uh, just that it seems that things go in cycles and life is no different. You know, like the Native Americans believed. A continuous, cyclic view of the world, instead of a linear one, with a beginning and end, like Western thought promotes."

"We come from dirt and return to dirt. That kinda stuff?" He was genuinely interested, but knew not why, and he had forgotten how she had just pinned him to the wall like a cheap calendar about their living situation.

"Well, sort of, I guess. That's part of it, I think. But, I mean more like *repeating* cycles."

"Huh? I still do not get what you mean by *cycles*. What goes around comes around? Karma?"

"Well, going through the same things over and over and over again, until you get it right, then you don't have to worry about it in life again, because you've already learned it. Yeah, kind of like Karma, I guess." She looked down at her hands, expecting some negative reaction from him.

In a few seconds, when it didn't come, she looked back up went on. "I've been reading this book about reincarnation. It's called "One More Time" and it outlines what the author thinks is how people choose to go through life after life after life and hopefully, learning as they go. It is based on some ancient Eastern thought of reincarnation, but it goes beyond that with a more modern interpretation."

He immediately and unconsciously rolled his eyes. "Oh, Buddhist voodoo shit. Nevermind."

She leaned forward and became stern, "Dave, don't patronize me! I'm serious! You need to find some way to reconnect with yourself, and everything else! You're such a beautiful and spiritual person when you can just be yourself." She was getting much more intense and Dave looked around to make sure that the other patrons were not paying them any unnecessary attention. They were not.

"Where did you hear about all this stuff?"

She took that jab personally. "Look, it might not be the end all answer to everything, but I think that there's something to it, like things happen for a reason, but we help to create our own reality through *our choices.*" Her voice was now a muffled chainsaw, full of teeth and one step from engaging and slicing.

He came back to seriousness when he saw how offended she got. *Wow! Really hit a frickin' nerve with that one.* "I'm sorry. Christy, really. I just didn't know that you went in for all that stuff." He quickly cleared his throat, *sure could use a cigarette now,* "I didn't think that you believed in *any* sort of religion. I mean, I know that you don't believe in 'God' so to speak, neither do I." After a pause. "I just thought that you were an Atheist."

She had calmed down. She responded very coolly, "Isn't that weird?"

Dave was surprised at the sudden change of her spirit, but gladly went with it. "What?"

"That we both met, in a country that is probably over 90% Christian, and both of us didn't believe in organized religion *of any kind?* I mean, we just assumed that was how it was, and for us it actually was."

"Yeah, but, lots of people hate religion nowadays." He thought that she was really reaching now.

"But there's a difference Dave, between religion and spirituality, right?"

"Sure. I guess so."

She could now see that she was getting nowhere. "Don't you ever wonder what there is, or *if* there is something, well,

I don't know, beyond this experience? Don't you ever feel like we've been here before?"

"The Lotus Garden?"

"You're such an asshole!" She pushed herself away from the table and began to scoot across the bench seat to leave. A few customers now looked up from their tables and Dave noticed them. "Get bent, Dave. I'll catch a cab."

Dave hurriedly tried to soften the situation. "No, please. Okay, okay. I'll drop it. I'm Sorry. I don't mean to sound condescending or anything."

She now saw that he was finally sincere. Dave had pushed the joke a little too far. "Love, I'm sorry. I really didn't mean to push your buttons. I just am not sure what it is that you're talking about, so I started to joke about it. You know I do that when I get lost in a conversation. It's one of my many self defense mechanisms." Dave smiled because he was actually calling himself on his own neurosis. Christy recognized it as well. He thought about blaming his mood and lack of enthusiasm on his job, but decided that might only open a bigger can of worms. Nope, tonight he was just an asshole.

Dave continued, "how about we eat?"

Christy could recognize a good exit line and she decided it really was time to just let it go for now. She slid back into the bench seat, in front of him, staring at him with those pure, timeless pools of jade. She grabbed his hands in hers and spoke very softly. "If you're really interested, even in just looking at the book, just looking through it, I'll leave it for you. It's in my bag, in the car."

"You have it in the car?" He caught himself and luckily she hadn't been offended by his tone. "Sure, Christy, I'll look at it." *Man, if it'll keep her chilled out for awhile, I'll read the entire Encyclopedia Britannica, cover to cover!*

He had another thought pop into his head. *Hey, we never even talked about me moving out of my place. As if I'm going to bring that topic up, especially right now.*

Christy responded, "All I am saying, is give the book a chance."

"You're starting to sound like John Lennon."

She smiled at his joke. "You'll like it, Dave. It really makes you think. It helps you kind of put things in some sort of spiritual perspective." She grabbed the serving spoon, put some veggie-fried rice on her plate and then grabbed a forkful and put it into her mouth. She mumbled through a mouthful of rice, "The food's still pretty warm and you have to have some of this rice."

"What? You think I'm really nice?" They both chuckled. Dave grabbed the other serving spoon, the one in the sweet and sour bean curd. He put some onto his plate and they switched spoons, then they finished grabbing their food. "So, whadaya say? Your place after dinner?" He gave her a charming smile, as if nothing had happened.

She responded to it well, realizing that the timing was wrong to say, *you mean, our place?* She had gotten him to open up some and he was even going to look into a book that she had recommended to him. He might not read the whole thing, but at least he'd look at it. Dave didn't read much these days; ESPN was much easier to digest. Christy thought, *round one, you win Christy.* "Dave, I hope you don't get too full on all this food. I've got plans for you later."

"Yeah?"

"Oh, yeah." She smiled.

After finishing the meal and then ordering and drinking two servers of hot, strong Saki, they returned to her townhouse. They raced up the stairs, pulled off their clothes, climbed into her queen bed, and tossed the fluffy faux down (real goose down is obtained too cruelly) comforter aside to the floor.

Christy clicked on a small CD player that was on her nightstand and then she turned off her small lamp that was also on the nightstand. It was a glass Tiffany lamp with a black metal frame. It had red roses painted delicately onto each separate tear drop shaped piece of clear glass: all of the points coming together in the center above the bulb, at the top of the lamp.

She turned back to Dave and gave him a strong kiss that warmed him from head to toe. He pulled back for a moment, brushed her hair aside, stared into her deep green eyes, and then he leaned into her for an even more powerful kiss. They fell into each other's arms and made passionate love, their caresses firm but sweet. They climaxed simultaneously. Then, they were quickly asleep on their backs, on top of the covers. Her CD player was still softly singing out John Lennon's immortal words, ". . . and we all . . . shine . . . on . . . like the moon, and the stars . . . and the sun . . ."

Outside of her townhouse, there was no moon and no wind. Stone gray clouds densely blanketed the evening sky. There were only a few rips revealing deep violet. The clouds made the night even darker. The only light was from the streetlamps; their amber glow hardly shown into Christy's room at all.

After an hour and a half of tossing and turning, Dave awoke. Christy was out cold, snoring lightly and drooling a little onto her pillow. Dave quietly laughed at this.

He couldn't get back to sleep. He felt restless, but with the weekend upon them, he didn't want to go back to his place. *How would that look, disappearing into the night after making love? Wham-Bam Thank you M'am? With my fiancé? No she wouldn't have any sense of humor about that.*

Dave kind of liked the idea of not hearing cars squealing by the window, or the whirring sirens of police cars and ambulances, or the sounds of two drunks fighting down the block because one wouldn't give the other his keys to drive his '67 El Camino home, all at three in the morning, shortly after the local dive bars within shouting distance of his apartment had closed for the night.

There was enough light in the room to see by, barely, so Dave carefully slid his legs off of the bed, stood up and then walked quietly out of the room, down the stairs, and to the living room. He heard the tick tock of her kitchen clock. It was a much smaller version of a wooden grandfather clock and it sat on top of the counter where a microwave might have been at someone else's home (no nuked foods at Christy's house, thank you.)

Dave plopped down on the ornately decorated big cushion couch, grabbing the remote control just before hitting the seat. He pointed it at the television, aiming past a few short, Central American ironwood carvings that were on the glass and dark wood coffee table. The twenty seven inch screen lit up from within the matching wood armoire; luckily, the hutch doors were left open, so he hadn't needed to get up again.

Dave immediately made sure that the volume would not blast. Christy didn't usually run her TV through the stereo system, unless there was a particular concert broadcast that she was interested in, something along the lines of Bob Dylan or Pink Martini. He was in luck.

He flipped through the channels. It had taken him a year to get Christy to trade in her rabbit ears for even just the most basic of cable television.

The usual late night shows appeared: an infomercial about making millions of dollars with no money down, a large lady in bright clothing asking for relief funds to help children in Africa, an evangelical preacher asking for donations so that God can have more disposable income, some random modern cartoons and Japanese animation, and a rerun of M.A.S.H. that was about half over. M.A.S.H. it was.

Colonel Potter was responding to Burns and Hoolihan about a complaint they had cooked up to get Pierce and Macintyre into trouble. Dave always hated Burns. Robert Duval was fine in the movie version, eventually he got carted away as a nut case, but the television's version of "Ferret Face" really got on his nerves. He thought, *I guess that's the point to his character; he's very well cast.*

Dave heard a noise like the wind gusting quickly and then light raindrops began to fall outside. He got up and peeked through the blinds of the front window. The mist was barely recognizable at ground level, but as he looked up he saw millions of tiny amber tinted prisms radiating down from around the bulb of the street lamp. They seemed to fall in perfect unison, leaving short rainbow trails behind them that quickly disappeared as they came closer to the ground. He watched for a moment, admiring the complexly organized beauty and rhythm of nature, then he grabbed a glass of milk, mixed in some chocolate syrup from the fridge. Christy's only real vice was dark chocolate. He then headed back for the couch.

Back on the show, Radar was telling Pierce in his high pitched voice that the nurse that he had been trying for was "going to be transferred," just as the wounded soldier he had previously operated on was "okay" and about to go home. *That's life. Win some, lose some.*

There was a commercial and Dave began to finally feel tired again. An instant came in and, as it often does, lasted much longer than an instant.

As with most late night television, there were several more commercials. Buy a Quick Cut mower. Curl your hair with the Hoopty Doo. Get car financing with bad or no credit. Dave's eyelids were sand bags and the strings holding them up were slipping.

He began to nod off just as Carl Sagan's "Cosmos" came onto the screen. His grip on the remote loosened from his hanging hand and it slid slowly toward the carpet. It hit noiselessly as the voice from the television was saying, "Billions and billions of stars . . . billions and billions of connections . . . billions and billions of possibilities . . ."

Dave slid into a deep sleep. After a few minutes of Dr. Sagan going on about how Mars could have once supported life and then going into the basic theory of worm holes and time travel possibilities, Dave's eyelids began to flutter. REM sleep. Dave was beginning to dream.

The images flashed behind his eyes. There was his Volkswagen with a new paint job and new Porsche hub caps. He suddenly smelled pizza; he could taste a milkshake, then French fries, then watermelon flavored sorbet. A fluorescent haze blotted out the smells and then it covered his vision. The pictures then fleeted in and out of the haze, insignificant and brief. Then, like a kaleidoscope clearing, the images became crisp.

Dave's mind is a racing blur. There are images of him in high school, playing baseball. He hears, "it's going, going . . . it's gone! Jones has done it again!" Then the image clouds over and he walks by an office at a college. He can't read the name on the door, it is blurred. It feels very familiar, but he doesn't remember ever being there before. He's sure he's been by it, but it's more than that. It seems like he belongs there. Some sort of connection? Something?

Carl Sagan opens the office door, his eyes are but vacant pools of obsidian black. Endless and eternal. Sagan says, "biiiiiiiiiiiillions and biiiiiiiiiiiiiillions of staaaaaaars . . . and eeeeev-en moooorrre . . . moooooooooorrrre thaaaaan youuuuuuu caaaaaannnnn immm . . . aaaa . . . ggggiine . . . feeeeeeeeel theeeee en-errrr-gyyyyy . . ."

The cotton candy clouds come back and swirl blue and green, then orange and yellow to clear and then they reveal a bright sunny day. Dave is much younger, in his mid teens. The smell of salt water hangs warm in the air. Palm trees waive their leaves happily and gently in the light wind, atop tall and slender stalks.

Dave leans down and touches a starfish, startling himself as much as the starfish. He hears, "Honk! Honk!" and then he looks up and sees a white BMW pulling away from the beach, the passenger is a beautiful blond woman. She looks very natural. The driver's face is hidden. For some reason, this scene makes him feel warm and happy.

He next sees a trashy looking brunette, wearing a 1930s house dress and shoes. Her hair is in bobby pins, and she is in a cheap, dilapidated one bedroom house. There is some sort of very old car, possibly a Model T? It is visible through the dirty screen on the opened front door. It is very hot and humid in this place. The woman is yelling at him, telling him that it's his fault that they can't pay the rent and it's a good thing that they don't have any kids. He knows that her name is Charlotte.

Dave sees that his hands are covered with grease. The woman calls him William and she screams what a useless, lazy, unmotivated piece of shit he is, and that she thinks she loved him once, that things don't always go your way, that money should be the first thing on his mind. She continues on for a moment about how she isn't properly taken care of and she always has deserved something better.

The man wants to hit her, wants to hit her badly, but he holds back. Dave knows that something isn't right. The man tells her that if she wasn't such a gold digger bitch, then they would be a lot better off. He'd be a lot better off. He shouts, "I'm an unemployed mechanic, what am I supposed to do?! Half of the country is out of work!" He goes on saying that it's her fault that they never had children and that her greed of always wanting more, more, MORE is what is driving them apart.

"Fuck you, you, you bastard!" That particular remark becomes muffled . . . distant . . . and is fading away. Dave thinks this argument seems so stereotypical. And yet, he can sense that those two should've made it. They should be happy together. She is the right one for him, he thinks, but the timing is off, or something. Maybe they're both not quite, the right people, yet? What the hell does 'yet' mean?

Dave knows the two will be divorced soon, but he can feel in his heart that it's not over. Her eyes, behind the pain, they're so warm. So strangely familiar. So . . . green.

Clouds suddenly swirl faster and faster, spinning him farther and farther. Dave feels the pressure of the spin, getting faster and faster, almost turning his stomach. The faster he goes, the rounder he gets.

He sees the beach again, far below him, slowly fading into black, as he is pulled forcefully away. He reaches for the sand, trying desperately to hold on to that memory, that little slice of innocent heaven.

A flash of ice blue lightning splits the sky and he is back sitting watching television at Christy's house. It is morning and the sun is shining through the window onto his face, caressing him with warmth and peaceful bliss. He knows that he is on Christy's couch, asleep sitting up, but he feels that he is back on the beach, sitting beside the tide pool, next to purple and orange starfishes, lost in a sunshine daydream of a wonderful yesteryear.

"Dave." *The ocean crashes in over him and the sand slowly erodes as the water pulls back into the ocean. There is the fuzzy crackle of static electricity.* The noise suddenly stops.

Click.

Dave opens his eyes to see that Christy is standing over him. She wears gray sweatpants and a t-shirt with an otter printed on it. "Hey Mr. Jones, good morning. What are you doing down here? How long have you been awake?" She was glad that he had actually stayed the night and not headed for his apartment.

Dave thought, *I'm awake?*

After Dave had awoken, he contemplated his dream. He wasn't sure what it all meant. He only knew that it was confusing and it left him with an eerie, familiar feeling for a little while. However, by the middle of the afternoon he couldn't remember most of the dream. He had begun to tell Christy about it over breakfast, but when she heard it, she brought up the book thing again. He quickly changed the subject to what she was currently doing with her kids at the elementary school. He was very subtle and she didn't notice his intentional shift of topics. He really was interested, but not so much at that moment. He thought, *dodged another bullet.*

The rest of the weekend had gone well, Dave and Christy electing to stay home on that rainy Sunday and watch a movie called, "Fools Rush In." It was a chick flick that starred Matthew Perry and Salma Hayek. In the movie, the couple falls in love and overcomes serious obstacles in both their personal and professional lives in order to be together. Of course, *he* had a great paying job and *she* was an artist, which made it a little cheesy. But, it was very soothing and allowed them both some much needed cuddle up on the couch and snuggle time.

Dave had gone to his apartment to sleep that night, so that he could get up and get ready for work. He had forgotten to stop by his place and pick up clothes for after the weekend and by the time he had remembered, it was late Sunday afternoon anyway. Christy put up a little bit of a fight, but she knew that Dave probably needed some time by himself and she guessed that she could use the time to prep for her work week as well.

Monday afternoon found Dave once again in his seat at the edge of the imaging center desk. Dana had called in sick and Betty was at lunch. Rochelle had to attend some two day training on the 'motivation of staff in difficult environments.' This seminar amounted to learning about how to force your subordinates to do more work, in the face of increasing responsibilities, heavier foot traffic flow and the addition of a new CT machine that would be running day and night to offset the costs of its installation, therefore bring in many, many more patients to check in and process for their examinations.

Of course, Rochelle would return with all of her nuggets of knowledge that meant absolutely nothing to anyone except for her and management. Her intentions were good, in that she really did want the company to be more profitable. It was just hard on the day to day workings of a staff that was already being pressed too thin, and of who would never see any of those increased profits.

The staff would do whatever it was that they needed to do in order to keep their jobs; they knew the score. The brown nose points for Rochelle, and any other management personnel for that matter, seemed to accumulate at a faster rate when these seminars were attended. She would get to go to the Hilton for two days, enjoy prime rib one day and cashew chicken the next, along with a continental breakfast on each of the days.

Besides, Human Resources had just told the support staff that there wouldn't be any funds available for bonuses this quarter, even though volume and profits were up, so it seemed like the perfect time for a supervisor to go to a two day, $3500 seminar.

The good news for Dave was that Rochelle was out of the office. While the workload wouldn't be any lighter, the tension was always much less when she was gone. And when you add in the fact that the mostly useless Dana had called in sick as well, things were actually moving along pretty quickly and more smoothly than usual. It was almost, *almost* fun for Dave to be there that day.

There was a slight lull in the action, so Candy and Dave began to slowly fold envelopes, trying to look busy. Candy said, "So, Dave, what's new with you?"

"Not too much, same ol', same ol'. What about you?" He looked up at the door, saw nobody, and returned to folding.

"Well, we just got a new car! It is a Subaru wagon. It is yellow with tan interior. I just love it!" Dave could hear the excitement in her voice, even though she spoke somewhat softly.

"That sounds pretty cool. Is it brand new?"

"Yup, right off the dealer's lot. We have been looking for a long time and this one finally came up. And, it was such a good price, we decided to take it." Candy's husband had recently gone back to work as a contractor and had been making some good extra money since coming out of semiretirement.

"I am kind of looking for something myself," Dave replied.

"Are you getting tired of that cute little Volkswagen?" She smiled, honestly thinking that his car was very cute.

"Well, I like it, but its super cold blooded in the winter and there really isn't much room to do anything with it."

"What kind of car are you looking for?" She looked up at the door. Some people walked up to read the doctor's names on the glass, but then they decided to move on down the hall. Dave and Candy's letter folding continued.

"I think I want a truck. You know, something a little older, so that the price is easier to swallow."

Candy replied, "A truck, huh? That sounds like you, Dave. I can see you driving up all cool and looking tough in your shiny new truck." She gave him another big smile, ribbing him a little bit.

Dave laughed, "I'll have to see what is out there. Maybe I'll pick up an "Auto Trader" or a "Car Shopper" or something like that. I'm not quite ready to go and get a new one from the dealer's lot."

"Sometimes the one's that have already been lived in are very nice."

"Well, with my budget, I can only hope for something that looks decent and still has some life left in it."

They folded letters until someone rang the buzzer for the door, signaling that the referring offices must have been back from their lunches. Candy whispered, "I hate it when they do that. Can't they check to see if the door is unlocked?"

Dave replied with a smirk, "apparently not." They both laughed and prepared to get back to the business of registering and processing the patients for their examinations.

CHAPTER 7

Dr. Kennedy Jones sat in his office on that Tuesday, reading the latest book in the Dark Tower series: "Wolves of the Calla." He had grown up reading Stephen King's novels and was particularly excited to know that the Tower series was finally completed. Dr. Jones' peers might have snuffed at King's work, but he knew better. He thought, *the canon is a bunch of crap anyway. What about Stephen King? What about a book like Jean Rhys' "Wide Sargasso Sea" that pokes fun at the canon and reeks of imperialistic irony against Jayne Eyre? What about Edward Abbey with his biting environmental commentaries in "The Monkey Wrench Gang," or the follow up, "Hayduke Lives?" What about all of the Fantasy writers keeping Medieval quests and dragons alive? Not to mention the entire catalog of international authors that only now are beginning to see the light of day in the American university studies programs.*

There were obviously some pieces of fiction that weren't as of yet recognized for their eloquent voices, simply because they didn't fit into the prescribed genre parameters. *To hell with them! I'm going to finish this Tower saga and then get hold of all seven books in hardcover first editions and then get Stephen goddamn King himself to sign them if I can. Then, I'll put them in my library for all to see. Right between Hunter S. Thompson's, "Fear and Loathing in Las Vegas" and J.R.R. Tolkien's, "The Hobbit!"* The thought of this made him excited. Oh the crusty theorists he would offend just by having them there!

The book came to a part where 'The Gunslinger,' Roland, helped his comrade, Eddie to travel through a door to another dimension; another "when" as King called it. This struck Kennedy as a source of limitless potential. *Wow! To be able to choose your own "when"; maybe your own "how" and "where" . . . just to be able to experience some other life existence possibility!*

The previous books had utilized these ghostly portals, but this one, book five, was the first time that the characters were able to guide their sense of "when" just by concentrating hard enough. Then a thought occurred to Kennedy. *What if everything was controlled by your sense of "why?" The choice to enter the portal, to go to a "when" in order to fulfill some sort of chosen destiny . . . or maybe even the next life. Whoa.*

Kennedy heard a knock against the wooden door of his office. The door was cheaply painted, a fading yellow, but had the solid sound of a long since departed sense of construction, a time when people actually crafted doors. *They don't make 'em like they used to.*

"Come in."

"Hey, Professor Jones. It's almost time for your three o'clock class." It was Kennedy's assistant, Dan. Dan was an MA candidate: a hard worker that spent a great deal of time exploring cultural endeavors, a.k.a. partying. He wore a faded "Phish" concert shirt beneath a nicer black long sleeved, collared shirt, unbuttoned and open. His jeans were faded, but not ripped. Dan's grades were always good and he seemed to be having fun. *He'll Probably make a good professor someday*, Kennedy thought.

"Thanks. I'm on it." Kennedy folded up his Stephen King and set him on the top of the small desk, next to the brushed silver desk lamp. "Until later, my universe saving friends," he whispered to himself.

"What's that Doctor Jones?"

"Sorry, *No time for love*, Dan."

"Excuse me, sir?" Dan clearly didn't catch the reference and was completely lost, hoping that this wasn't some strange come on or something.

"Indiana Jones? Ring a bell? Yes? No? Never mind. I'll be down in a minute."

"Sure, Dr. Jones. Whatever you say."

Dan was relieved. He'd seen Indiana Jones, well, parts of it he had thought, on TBS or something, at 2:00am, after several beers, but that didn't matter. He'd clearly missed the quote, but he was glad that it was only a quote and nothing more.

Dan got a little high strung around Dr. Jones. He was not so much intimidated, but it was more of a sense of extreme respect for the weird, nice guy who was so smart and intuitive. He never could call him Kennedy, although he had been asked to a few times in the past. Dan would probably always refer to him as, "Dr. Jones."

For having such an outgoing personality, Kennedy maintained a very private and controlled home life. It was a little odd to a good many people that Kennedy had never married. He never really dated much either. Occasionally, he could be seen out to dinner with a pretty lady, more often than not a colleague of some sort, but that was all it ever was.

A few suspected that he was gay. Sometimes he displayed somewhat flamboyant mannerisms, mainly when he got excited, and this further reinforced their assumptions. Kennedy was a very handsome and compassionate man, looking much younger than his actual age and he was very successful in his own right; he'd published one textbook as well as a few long works of fiction.

Many of his women coworkers at the University had remarked, out of his earshot of course, how Kennedy would make such an excellent father. But, it was like he was content to live with Emily, his cat, and to go on about his life just the same way he had been for years.

Kennedy was definitely not a homophobe, but never had been interested in men sexually or romantically, not in the least. He really didn't have that many friends, male or female. For some reason, being alone seemed to be better for him. He just wouldn't open up to a woman. There was some scar, some internal barrier that he hid behind. It was like an electric fence that sensed intimacy. Too close and BZZZZT! Game over. But of course, such an intelligent man did not show this side of himself. He kept on with his stasis, he threw himself into his work and he sailed on what appeared to most people to be very calm waters.

Maybe that is what got to Dan, the fact that Dr. Jones always seemed to be doing just fine, even keel, no stress, and couldn't be ruffled. Dan thought that if all the professors were like that, that on their game all of the time, then he'd better stop schooling after his Masters. Of course, having been in school so long already, Dan knew different.

Kennedy grabbed for his briefcase that was lying next to the office desk. He wasn't wearing a sport coat today, but adorned more of a formal looking Hawaiian print shirt. Fridays were always more of a casual day; however, Kennedy never began to look too relaxed until a little further into the term. He liked to wear the Hawaiian shirt during the second or third week of class, just to throw off the new students. If he thought he could get away with it once, just once, he'd wear a tie dye shirt, cut off shorts and Birkenstocks to class. Of course, that's not the right example to set. Eccentric is one thing, unprofessional is another. But today, his loud shirt was complimented by new black Dockers and some nice hiking shoes that he had recently picked up; the shoes being designed with all man made materials, of course.

Dan trailed off down the hall talking to himself, relieved, but still trying to figure out the quote. He'd be asking his friends as they all sat around the bong that weekend what this "No time for Love" stuff was all about and one of them might even know. Dan might even go rent the movie, just to find out.

Kennedy followed shortly after Dan, locking the copper colored doorknob on his way out. He walked down the hall, hearing his footsteps bounce off of the hard tiled floors and then again off of the textured walls, creating a short, hollow echo if one were to pay close enough attention.

By early afternoon, there were many less people in the hallways. They were mostly graduate students scrambling to their assistantships, or professors trying to get their grading done so as not to drag it home and a few others reading or heading to the library for research.

On such a nice day, most of the students were sprawled across the large and well manicured courtyard lawn, and they were wearing bright summer clothes and tossing Technicolor Frisbees, smoking clove cigarettes, drinking canned soda or iced lattes, or just lying on their backs with their books covering their faces from the smiling middle September sun. The sun that seemed warmer and stuffier than it had in August. The sun that had only been back for a few short, precious months. The same sun that would soon turn and run with its golden rays in hand, hoarding them into hiding for another six or seven months deep behind thick clouds, only to give way to the cool breezes, and then the hard, cold rain.

Kennedy approached the open door of his classroom, carrying his briefcase under his arm and seeing several students seated in larger, adult versions of the typical grade school, one piece desks. The desks were uncomfortable, but they did the trick for an hour and a half, twice a week. Of course, Dr. Kennedy Jones' chair, sitting tucked behind an older wooden desk, was somewhat nicer. The kicker was that he hardly ever got to sit in it.

Kennedy looked out across the tired faces of twenty five or so students, as he walked over to the desk, set down his briefcase, opened it and pulled out a thick literature book. The cover was worn, but the pages were in perfect condition. A few of the bodies in the audience showed a spark of actual interest, but mostly they were just a wash of pallid, dissociated blankness.

The early morning courses were tough enough to teach, but most students had discovered Starbucks, or the really hip crowd would go to Allan Brothers for their black bean fix. Students were usually sort of human within fifteen minutes. By the afternoon, the wiring buzz had long since worn off, the heaviness of lunch was pressing down and most students would rather take a nap than listen to someone drone on about Chaucer or Shakespeare or, if they were lucky, the favorite local resident, Ken Kesey.

No such luck today, though. Kennedy greeted the class with, "Good afternoon. I'll be on page 375 of the anthology, if you care to follow along." He looked up for a moment and then turned to the page in his book. As he turned around he continued, "of course, this *will* be on the mid term." At that point, several books quickly snapped open. He waited for a second, heard the rustle of notebooks and pencils and then began to read from "Paradise Lost," thinking the whole time, *they can be sleepy if they choose to, but THIS-IS-MY-JOB.*

Kennedy went on flawlessly and read the section of the story as animated as anyone could possibly read one of Milton's dry works. Some things were required curriculum, even at a university. But, the students had no clue that Kennedy found Milton boring, or that he thought that Milton's jokes were terrible and that they didn't translate well into the modern world.

His teaching day had gone along fine, with the exception of Jasmine Delgado falling asleep face down and then waking herself up when her own drool oozed from the desktop and squished onto her cheek. The mousy squeak and subtle jerk she made was barely noticeable; nonetheless, he had noticed. She had perfected a way of hiding behind her long, curly black hair. He knew that she had faded out before. But, she kept up her grades, so he figured that he had no reason to razz her. This wasn't high school. She was paying to be there, for one reason or another.

By the end of the day, Kennedy felt a little tired and he thought it best to skip his jog for the day. Whenever he could, he tried to run about five miles. When the rains came, most of his running was done on a treadmill at the Student and Faculty Fitness Center (SFFC). Still, he was generally pretty consistent about keeping his three or four times per week running quota active. He had gained a few pounds when he hit thirty, but he had managed to remove it quickly with the running. So far, between a vegetarian diet, minimizing sweets and running fairly often, he had kept in pretty good shape.

At least now he was home. Within a few minutes he'd have his usual glass of Cabernet; *keeps the arteries clean*. When finished, he would head upstairs to his bedroom and dive back into his Stephen King book. *The Gunslinger waits for no one.*

Earlier in the day, when he first packed the hardback book into his canvas briefcase, he had thought about driving up to the lake. It could be one of the few truly nice days left for the year. But, he thought it best that he didn't go. After the last experience up there, *whatever the hell that was*, he might be better off to just head for home. For relaxation. For his own sanity.

After finishing up his dinner and heading upstairs, he sat up in bed, his back against the dark bed frame, his lower back supported by one of his pillows. His mind was restless and uneasy.

Occasionally he'd get these types of feelings. Feelings of loneliness, feelings of emptiness, feelings of lacking, feelings of regret and missed opportunities. Of course, it was only at home, at night, in the confines of his own sanctuarial house, that he would dare acknowledge such underpinnings. This was the only time that he might allow some vulnerability to surface and only to a very consoling, and purring, Emily.

Kennedy took a deep breath and sighed, thinking about a girl he knew in high school, feeling somewhat sorry for himself. She was beautiful. He had really liked her. Her name was Ashley.

Ashley lived in the small country town of Livermore, out in the valley, just East of the Bay Area. Kennedy and Ashley had been very close friends and did many things together; spending time on the beach, eating shakes and fries at the corner Dairy Queen and talking on the phone for hours at a time about life and whatever else came into their teenage minds.

One time, they had spent the weekend at the San Francisco Blues Festival. They had parked near the water in her early 1970s, orange, VW Vanagon Camper. They watched the outdoor shows that included incredible performances by both local talent and big named players like B.B. King and John Lee Hooker. The shows were on both Friday and Saturday, from early afternoon and they continued on into the night. That Saturday had been extra special, though. After smoking pot and sipping Mexican beer all day, surrounded by very friendly, countless strangers, they returned to the van for some dinner and cards before hitting the hay. Ashley lit some Nag Champa incense, *still his favorite*, and then they fired up the propane stove and prepared a curry and veggie stir-fry, boiling water for the jasmine rice. She even added a little saffron. Kennedy was not a vegetarian at that point in his life, but he always enjoyed her cooking because she could cook well and she was the only vegetarian that he knew. Actually, that meal was now still one of his favorites that he would cook for himself.

After the meal, the two of them got out the cards. The deck was a specially designed Grateful Dead deck. Instead of the traditional hearts, clubs, spades and diamonds, there were suns, moons, wheels and roses in their places. The face cards were intricately drawn as well, with each of the characters being cleverly replaced by skeletons. The cards came with a special release packaging for the CD, "Built to Last."

The Vanagon windows were open, the tiny, now dusty, screens letting in the salty sea air and the sound of the occasional sloshing of the Bay against the dock. The two of them sat sipping a Napa Valley cabernet, curiously, another one of his all time favorites, as they played to win at Hearts.

"What did you think about the show today," she asked him.

"I really liked Johnny Lee Hooker."

"Yeah, me too. Who was that Bessie Smith sounding lady?"

"I'm not sure, but she was great! Although she was a little too skinny to be like Bessie."

Ashley laughed and then replied, "That old style blues is really something when you can hear it live. She had such force in her voice."

"Especially at bayside, with the salt air and light ocean breezes . . . you can't ask for a better time."

"Ab-so-lutely." She smiled as she replied and then she took another sip of the tasty bittersweet red wine.

The night had slowly gotten colder, but the sea air was too refreshing to close the windows. Kennedy moved over to Ashley and held her in his arms. They had sat like this many times before, on a beach, at the park, watching TV, or after a San Francisco Giants game at Candlestick Park, which was always cold in the evening. She hadn't been much of a sports fan at all, but she did begin to really enjoy watching the Giants play because of Kennedy's passion for the team and for baseball in general. Kennedy had been such a die hard San Francisco Giants fan for his entire life that his enthusiasm had converted Ashley. In fact, she started keeping up on the team and even surprised him once in awhile by knowing something about a trade or some other happening with the team before he even knew about it.

However, this time the situation between the two of them somehow felt different. At that particular moment in time, Kennedy thought that it seemed more intense, but in a good way. Ashley sensed it too. They were a pulling of magnets, some sort of energy exchange that was far too big for either of them to resist. The stars had correctly aligned like cogs in a lock and they were now becoming two halves of the same whole.

Ashley cocked her head and looked up into Kennedy's sea blue eyes. He stared back into her seductive, deep green eyes as he gently brushed her long, flowing hair back from her face. He thought, *such beauty*. His pulse quickened.

"Ashley," he whispered.

"Yes?" She replied softly.

"I . . . Just . . ."

They embraced in a passionate kiss and fell onto the (now folded out) bed. They kissed softly, lightly touching each other, like they had been together a million times before. The bay lapped against the docks rhythmically and the seagulls occasionally cried softly in the distance. There were no other noises and the people of The City had returned to their homes, or continued out for a night on the town. The two of them were together, without distraction, enveloped in the romance of a bayside San Francisco evening.

The couple's rhythm and intensity increased with a mixture of soft and firm caresses. They made passionate and strong love, again and again, feeling completely free and yet totally connected to each other. They then fell asleep in each other's arms with him curled around her and the ocean breeze gently cooling their naked bodies. Neither one felt ashamed or awkward. On the contrary, they felt at peace with the world, like one continuous energy.

That night of star crossed love was a defining changing point, but not in the way that Kennedy had expected it to be. It was one of the last times that he ever saw Ashley and it was the very last time that he ever felt that special electrical charge of connectivity with her, or any other woman for that matter.

They didn't speak for a few days and then it was back to the normal friendship that they had had previously, well sort of, but their friendship had weakened. They found themselves seeking things to talk about and they always seemed in a hurry to get off of the phone. The two did hang out together a few more times, going to a concert once and on another day to the beach. But, that wonderful, special friendship came quickly to a close. Ashley eventually had gone off to pursue a business degree at an East Coast university. Kennedy had remained on the West Coast to continue his education.

Something had changed over the course of a few months since that night and Ashley seemed to be very worried about her financial future and being secure. Looking back, it seemed that it had been slowly coming on before that miraculous evening, but maybe for some reason, that night was the catalyst that pushed her into play. Kennedy had come to attribute her change to when Ashley's father had gotten laid off from the San Francisco Chronicle, a few weeks prior to their romantic encounter. Ashley's father, Abe, had been an artist doing political cartoons and things of that nature for over 22 years, commuting well over an hour each way on a BART train and a bus and working nights in The City. His lay off put a lot of strain on her family, but she wouldn't talk about it. Never. At first she tried to play it off like it didn't affect her in the least. Then, she just got more quiet and more distant from everyone, especially Kennedy.

One day, Ashley snapped. She quit her volunteer work with the Boys and Girls Club of America and took on two nearly full time jobs. She said that the money was for college, but there seemed to be another reason for her actions. Besides, her grandparents had already agreed to pay for any college she got into, for four years, to cover her room, board and tuition, as long as she maintained a 'B' average. They had been saving for her since she was born. Unfortunately, her grandparents were not rich and could not otherwise help the family to compensate for Abe's lost wages.

The last time Kennedy had seen Ashley, she had cut her hair shorter, but still had looked somewhat like a "Hippy" or a "Granola." The main difference was that now she desired the $800 patchwork dress bearing the Nordstrom label, instead of one that was authentically hand stitched and then sold for a much lower price tag at a market, or from one of the vendors outside a show.

He had recently heard from a mutual friend that she was running some cosmetic company and working eighty hours a week to support her expensive spending habits. She lived in a high security building in one of the larger Eastern cities, probably in Boston or New York.

Kennedy, of course, had pursued an English and Journalism degree. He had wanted a chance to better perfect his writing talents. He kept writing and kept going to school, excelling in both.

There was a part of him that couldn't believe Ashley's change into a 'material girl.' He knew he was being judgmental and he didn't want to seem holier than thou, but it just didn't make sense to him. *That's not the Ashley I knew. What happened to the girl who used to tie dye t shirts and work with children? I mean, everyone gets a little more conservative when they get older, but she had talked about running a tea shop, not a cosmetics store.*

Kennedy had always thought that the two of them would get together and stay together, even before they had ever been physically intimate. He wasn't waiting for her, especially knowing how she had changed, but he hadn't met anyone else that could bring about that spark, or that calming sense of interconnected satisfaction. Kennedy knew that his ideas were romanticized and idealistic, yet it was as if the world ceased to spin at that moment in his life, at that one perfect time with her. A true oneness had radiated between and engulfed them. *How I miss that . . . that sense of unity. That sense of Oneness.*

Kennedy would date occasionally, mostly out of physical necessity, but it was never more than emotionless sex and then it was always over immediately after he and "Bachelorette Number 2" had finished. Luckily for him, being a charming and handsome man, he had a knack for drawing busy, single, professional women toward him that were after the same thing; no strings, no guilt, no worries. It worked out for the both of them every time and there had never been any sort of complications.

Sometimes, he would just sit alone in his house and think about his life. Sure, he was happy and satisfied professionally, but what about a relationship? *Could there really be only one person that is meant for each of us? Is that what I've become? Someone who tells himself that he has everything, but in reality lacks the most important piece? Why doesn't anyone else ever feel right to me? Was that it? My one and only shot? Am I destined to be alone?*

Sure, biologists tell you that we are compatible with any number of other human beings, it just becomes a matter of what we are willing to compromise on. We are only born to reproduce and propagate the Earth with our offspring, so that they can go out when they are old enough and keep the cycle going. Survival of the Species at its best. That sounded good on paper, but it didn't work in reality for Kennedy. Biology was one thing, but the intense energy and esotericism of true love was another.

Realizing that his questions would not be answered that night, Kennedy lay down and closed his eyes. He felt Emily jump up onto the bed, which startled him at first, but then he quickly fell asleep with her curled up next to him.

The rest of the work week had gone well and Dr. Jones was really getting the feeling that he was one of the professors, not just an assistant anymore, but one of the permanent fixtures at the University of Oregon. With full tenure, he felt more secure than at any position that he had ever worked in. It felt good to him.

He was assigning papers, grading them, giving articulate, cogent and interesting lectures, staying after class for tutoring students, having the occasional beer with Dan and doing his running a few times a week. Kennedy was in the full swing of the Fall Term and things couldn't be better for him.

When Friday came, he went home immediately after his last class, electing to begin his weekend a little early. He had seen someone earlier in the day that had reminded him of a young Ashley, and the thoughts of her filled his mind all afternoon. He wouldn't believe that she had changed so much from the person he used to know. She just couldn't be a gold digger. There had to be something more to it than that. He thought, *should I try to look her up? Try to use my research abilities to find an address or a phone number? Turn in to Columbo for the day?* He knew where to look and he also knew that it would only be a matter of an hour or so and then he could contact her and find out about her first hand.

He thought, *Jesus! Now you're about to stalk someone you haven't seen in several years! What if she's gotten married and has kids? How's that going to look Mr. New Professor?* He decided that it wasn't such a good idea; however, that night he ate a dinner of tofu and jasmine rice, with saffron, while sipping on some Napa Valley cabernet wine.

CHAPTER 8

Dave sat and stared at his eggs, knowing that he had awoken from an intense dream, but barely remembering any of it. He knew that there was something about a heated argument and an old car, in some dusty Southern town, but that was about it.

The smell of Kona coffee and vegetarian bacon filled the kitchen. Christy finished placing some organic cantaloupe onto her plate and went over to sit at the table, across from Dave.

She asked, "Is everything okay Baby? You seem kinda quiet." She went back to slicing her melon.

"What, oh yeah, I'm great. I just had a dream."

"Really, what was it about?"

"I don't remember much, but it was very intense." He began to think about his food.

"Intense, how? Was I in it?" took a drink of orange juice.

"No, no, nothing about you, I don't think." He suddenly remembered the couple arguing in his dream.

"You don't *think*?" Now, Christy was beginning to become curious.

"I mean, I don't really remember. Maybe it'll come to me later. If it does, I'll let you know." He took a bite of the veggie bacon, and then took a drink of his orange juice.

"Okay, but if I'm in it, it better be good. I want a starring role in all of your dreams." She smiled.

"Yeah, all right." Dave was distracted, and Christy could tell.

"You know, that book I lent you might talk about this dream stuff . . ." She had said it before she realized it.

Dave concealed an annoyed look and changed the subject to her work. Christy gladly took the bait and forgot about his dream instance. For the moment, she rambled on about Elementary education and the state mandated tests that she thought were an unfair way to check for student achievement.

Christy hadn't always been so in touch with spirituality. In fact, she had renounced her Catholic upbringing when she was 14, shortly after her first communion. Her mother Rosemary, with whom she was extremely close, had been hit and killed by a drunk driver a few months before that. It was all she could do to go through with the communion ceremony, but Christy felt like she owed it to the rest of her family.

Russell, Christy's father, had never really tried to reach out to Christy. With Rosemary gone, Christy became more of someone that he tolerated than loved. He did what he had to. He provided food, shelter and clothing, but no love. He didn't even care that she quit Catholic school and opted for public education. Russell was playing the role until Christy turned 18.

Rosemary had been blessed with beautiful green eyes, the eyes that shined emerald and lit up Russell's heart from their first meeting. Following Rosemary's accident, when Russell saw those very same eyes looking back at him from within the face of his daughter Christy, it was like she was pouring salt into his wound. It was more than he could stand. Rosemary was his world, his only one, and she always would be. Losing that connection with her was too much for him to handle and he lost it completely. He immediately and sharply distanced himself from his only remaining connection to his deceased wife, his daughter Christy.

Of course, a young Christy never understood why her father acted this way towards her and she had actually thought that they would at least have each other to make it through the loss of Rosemary. Christy eventually knew that when her mother died, she really lost both of her parents. She was truly alone.

It was at that point, Christy changed her thoughts on faith into believing that there was no God, and then she was repulsed by the idea that she could've ever believed in some omniscient white male, with a beard, who died for our sins and dictated what the entire universe was doing at any given time. She thought, *absolutely ridiculous.*

Luckily, Christy had maintained her grades using education as fuel for her fire to leave home. She not only kept up her studies, graduating cum laude, but she read incessantly. By the time she was a high school senior, she was well versed in Plato, Aristotle, Socrates, Nietzsche, Ginsberg, Kerouac and even the lyrical analysis of Bob Dylan's songs. The reading allowed for her temporary escape, and she needed a lot of escape time at that point in her life.

However, such philosophical enlightenment came at no small cost to her social life. She was a recluse and had very few friends, at least very few that even tried to understand her. She was the weirdo, the one that cheerleaders and jocks poked fun at behind her back to further inflate their own egos and help them to deeply bury their own insecurities. It was not until her studies at The University of Oregon, where she met Dave, that she had found more of the people who thought somewhat similarly to what she believed. The U of O was a strong research institution, but maintained equally as strong of liberal arts education programs. Here is where she further studied philosophical concerns, but also opted to pursue art, literature, Eastern religious studies, Tai Chi and meditation while earning her Bachelor's degree and her Elementary teaching credential.

She had become a teacher, a person of influence. She had a direct affect on the lives of others and was good at it. She liked it and felt that it was her calling. For the first time in her life, things started to make sense. She felt that she was now at the point where she was moving along in the right direction. She had broken free from her father's damnation, and she was in control of her own destiny. And then there was Dave.

The day she met Dave, it was raining. It was the first day of a new quarter in early January. Dave was standing outside of a classroom, having a cigarette underneath a black umbrella. When Christy stepped out of her car, Dave saw her covering her hair with a green plastic notebook. She looked up and saw Dave standing there and smoking, but she had more pressing issues on her mind. *Why the hell can't I find my umbrella?*

Dave tossed his smoke down into a puddle. It sizzled for a brief moment and then was out. He walked over toward Christy as she quickly walked toward the classroom. He met her about halfway and offered to share his umbrella. Even with her wet hair that was mussed and plastered to her head, he thought she was beautiful. She looked up at him once she was under his portable canopy. Her green eyes gave him a joyful chill that made him feel that he could swim in them for eternity. She said, "Thanks."

"Oh, don't worry about it. I wished I'd have seen you before you got so soaked." He paused for a second then said, "I guess this wet weather is why they call us the Oregon Ducks." They shared a quick laugh and then they began to make their way to the classrooms.

They walked slowly, huddled together and keeping dry as best as they could. She asked, "What's your name?"

"Dave. And you?"

"Christy."

"Hey, are you headed to the Nietzsche class?"

"No, actually, I'm headed to Eastern Religions. It is in room A-47." She was beginning to relax. Beginning to forget just how drenched and cold she was.

"Yeah, I've taken a few other philosophy courses and this one seemed like it would be interesting." He was trying to not stumble over his words. He was coming off very smoothly on the outside, but his interior was shaking like a ninety year old woman who just downed ten cups of black coffee. "What about you?"

"I've taken my share." They walked into the covered area in front of the classroom. She asked, "Where is your class?"

He folded up his umbrella. "I'm across the breezeway in A-49." He paused for a second, and then reached in to his pocket. "Hey, we've got a few minutes. You want a smoke?"

"No thanks, I've never been much of a smoker. It doesn't bother me if you do, though." She smiled as she used her hands to squeeze some of the water from her hair. She stood up and tossed her hair back. "How do I look?" she asked humorously.

Dave lit the cigarette, took a drag and as he let out the smoke he replied, "Maaahvelous Dahlink." Her smile got a little bigger. He was trying to blow the smoke away from her. "You sure this smoke isn't bugging you? I can put it out."

"Not at all. Sometimes I really miss the smell. My father . . ." She paused for an instant remembering a time before her mother had passed on, and then continued, "That sounds kind of weird, doesn't it?" She looked down to the ground for a second, then back at him.

"Makes perfect sense to me. My Great Grandfather used to smoke Pall Malls without the filter. It was the stinkiest thing ever, always on his clothes, in his car, you know. But, I *really* miss that smell sometimes. Even though I couldn't smoke those harsh things, it's nostalgic, in a weird kind of way."

"Nostalgic, yeah, that's a good way to put it." She looked at the large Big Ben style clock across the street at the Administration Building.

Dave said, "Well, about that time, huh?"

"Yeah. Well, Dave, nice to meet you." She extended her hand. He reached out and shook her hand. "Maybe I'll see you around?"

He replied, "Yeah, that would be great, uh, um, I mean." He stopped. The old lady mannerisms were manifesting on the surface.

"You *mean*?" Now she was curious. She found Dave attractive, despite the smoking thing, and he had been quite chivalrous, but she was ready to let it go and get to class before she was late.

He quickly recomposed himself. "Are you seeing anyone?" Inside he recoiled, preparing for the punch. Expecting the old, *well, my boyfriend is . . . do you know him? He plays football for . . . or, he is a manager at blah, blah computer firm . . .*

Dave did just fine with the ladies, but there was something about this one. He couldn't explain it, but he could feel it.

Something almost propelled him over to her with his umbrella, like he couldn't help it. He felt like a little boy inside.

"I'll tell you what, Dave. Here's my number." She pulled a partially damp page from her notebook and a pen from the metal spiral of its binding. She wrote it down, folded it up and handed it to him. She said, "Call me sometime," then turned and walked into A-47. After a couple of steps, she turned and said, "Oh yeah, thanks for the umbrella," and then she smiled and continued walking.

He replied, "Anytime." But, she was already walking through the door of her classroom.

That was how it began. He called her a few days later, even though he had wanted to call her that night. *I can't call too soon, can't seem too anxious*. They had only become closer since that day. They found that they shared the same tastes in music and even had taken many of the same courses. They were very compatible and he treated her very well with his attentive nature. His intellectual sense of humor was a breath of fresh air for her. Not to say that he couldn't be as silly as the situation called for. She began to think that he might be *the one* and when she really thought about it, she had felt that way since she gave him her phone number on that rainy winter's day, weird as it seemed. It *was* like love at first sight. She too had felt the connection, almost like she intentionally had left her umbrella at home that day. The strange thing was that when she returned home on that January day, the umbrella was in plain sight in the kitchen table.

But lately, things had been different. Dave had been different, since she graduated and took the teaching position. The spark had gradually left his eyes and he had chiseled his way into a rut. When his aspirations of being a top notch journalist or novelist didn't immediately flourish, he became bitter.

Dave had been stuck at what he viewed as a dead end reception job for over two years, with absolutely no chance of advancement within the company, ever. Since graduating, he hadn't been able to even land an internship with any kind of media organization. He sent out countless resumes and portfolios to news stations, newspapers, magazines, alternative publications, technical writing companies, sports broadcasting agencies, and even several positions that were listed as an "Administrative Assistant," thinking that it might get him in the door through producing the company's newsletters. Then, maybe, with some luck, he could move into marketing or writing copy for advertising. Any of those would have been more fulfilling than wasting away in an imaging center with no chance of ever moving past his current position, or pay level. He felt that he was destined to be the most educated medical receptionist in history. In his defense though, Eugene, Oregon was full of PhDs who tended bar.

Christy often secretly wondered if Dave had really applied himself. Sure, he had applied to literally hundreds of positions over the last few years, but *did he really go out looking? Did he go knock on the doors of the news stations and newspapers? Did he try to utilize all of his connections through the university?* She knew he had tried very hard, no doubt about that, she'd seen it firsthand, with all of the cover letters and applications he had taken hours upon hours to put together. She thought, though, that sometimes life was a matter of being in the right place, at the right time. Apparently, he hadn't been able to line things up correctly so that they just fell into place. It was almost like having the wrong attitude going into the application would jeopardize the right vibe from coming his way to open that door.

There was one thing recently that had really gotten to her. Dave was afraid to move in together, even though they were engaged to be married. This made no sense to her. He kept saying it was financial in nature, but she often wondered if it was just a way to keep from breaking out of his familiar little world of pity and depression. *Moving in with her just might set things in motion for him, and then what? What would he do if he really had the chance to succeed? What then?*

It seemed so clear and simple to her. Once he chose to accept his life for what it was and then quit wasting the time he'd been given, then things would begin to work out for him. *Didn't any of those philosophy classes ever sink in with him?* She really believed it, whether you called it karma, energy, or just plain *making your own good luck.* She was really beginning to see it. It was all making sense. Life was the experience, its own heavenly reward. *If you sit and stew about shit, that's what you get, shit. What did Bob Marley say? "A mighty god is a living man . . ."*

She would do what she could to help him see. Of course, she naturally wanted to help the man she loved out of this stagnation, but it was more than that. There was a bond that transcended their current situation. She felt something else too. Somewhere deep in her soul, she knew that she owed it to him, for something that they both might be a part of, someday.

CHAPTER 9

The sun came through Dave's open apartment window and hit a spherical prism that he had hanging on a piece of thick thread just inside the blinds. The tiny rainbows covered the walls. As the breeze slowly and gently turned the crystal, the bright colors danced about carelessly. The light moved seamlessly, in perfectly complemented harmony with every other piece. The light was bright, beautiful, and peaceful. The light seemed like it could hold all of the answers, like it was some sort of refracted omniscience.

Dave thought a lot about what Christy had said that previous night at dinner and had even taken a look through the book, *One More Time*. He thought it would read like L. Ron Hubbard's, *Dianetics,* like it would be a book that was basically a pep talk disguised as "self help" or some baloney like that. But once he began reading it actually made him more curious, because it started to make sense.

He sat on the worn but comfortable golden and green couch, his black Converse high tops laid upon the glass top coffee table, holding up his denim covered legs. The radio was turned down low and was playing classic rock. He'd told Christy that he needed to get some laundry and house cleaning done, but he would be back later on in the evening. He had actually started a load of laundry. Having a washer and dryer hook up in the apartment was a major benefit.

He browsed through the book, returning to the first chapter. It began by asking the question, "Have you ever known about something before it has happened?" He immediately thought of the 1-900 psychics that had infomercials on the late night television. That one made him chuckle slightly. The laughter wasn't necessarily in mockery, though. When he was younger, that sort of thing happened to him on a daily basis. When he was a teenager, he had taken for granted that he would dream about something or sense it a day or more before it happened, or realize that he had went through the exact same motions previously. He thought it all to be circumstantial, but he began writing down dreams in a journal when he had something he thought might be applicable in the future.

Of course, most of the time, when he had one of these visions, it *had* been previously written in his journal some time before. It was like he was connected to some cosmic broadcast that he inadvertently tuned into ever so often. Somehow, he could watch the future channel and gain insight into things before they ever happened. Though the things seem random in their nature and completely unrelated, Dave knew somehow there was a connecting thread that ran between all of them.

His mother, Janey, had frequently told him of her "premonitions" and that she had just always thought of herself as having Extra Sensory Perception or ESP. One of her premonition stories that she would tell about her youth took place when she was nine years old, living in a rural part of upstate New York. She lived on a small farm that had a deep well near the edge of the property. The well was always covered by a heavy, solid wood lid that was fastened tightly for safety reasons when the well was not in use. She always walked across the wooden cover of the well and believed that it somehow brought her good luck.

One particular humid summer evening, she was coming home at dusk. The smell of lilacs was intoxicating and the setting summer sun was casting a deep orange hue through the leaves of the tall sugar maples and weeping willows. She knew she had to be home soon for supper, because it was already very hard to see clearly through the mix of filtered light and shadows.

When Janey got near the well this time, she closed her eyes, as she always did before crossing, and took a big step toward the well. Suddenly in mid step, she got a cold chill and stopped. Then, she felt a single ray of the sunlight touch her cheek and calm her. After that brief second, for some reason, she decided to walk around the well instead of crossing over it directly. This was the first time that she had ever avoided crossing the well's lid. She skipped home quickly, singing, "Daisy, Daisy, Tell me your answer true . . ."

About ten minutes after she got home, while the family was gathered at the old wooden kitchen table eating a dinner of pot roast, baked potatoes and boiled carrots, one of the neighbors showed up at the back screen door. He yelled in to Janey's father, "Don, mind if'n I come in for a sect'?"

Her father answered, "Nah, come awn en, Jim." Jim, a large man, was your typical Northeastern farmer, denim overalls and all. He carried a large, red metal plumber's wrench at his side. His hands had streaks of grease on them. Jim pushed open the door and lumbered on in, his work boots hitting heavy on the worn linoleum with each step. When Jim got a little closer to the table, Janey's father continued, "Ya Hungury, Friend?"

"Nope, I et a bit ago. Anywho, I'm not here fer da food. What I wunted ta tell ya wuz, that there well of yours, uh, well, I saw it ain't covered up when I was a comin' over. So, I pulled that there wood top ya made back onta it and a strapped it down and locked it fer ya too." Janey's mother, Grace, looked up for a second at her husband and then subtly shook her head disapprovingly as she leaned back into cutting a bite of her pot roast.

"Waddn't covered? I thought I member'd coverin' it after I drew up some water for 'dem carrots we wuz boilin'."

"Well, It wadn't cover'd when I got to there, Don." He took off his faded New York Mets baseball cap and wiped the sweat off his forehead with the forearm of his flannel shirt. "I jus' din't want nobody a gittin I killed cuz a fallin' in that ol' thing. It'd be a sonofabitch to fall in 'der and we'd prolly nevah git 'em back up."

"Nah, Nah, I appreashate it. I'll 'ave to start to double check my double checkin', I rekon." The two of them let out a little laugh.

Jim said, "Well, gotta git myself home. I just wunted to return the rinch I borr'd 'dis mornin'." Jim set the large wrench on the table. It looked like a child's toy in his thickly muscled and hairy hand. Then he turned and headed toward the screen, opened it gruffly, put his hat back on, and walked out and down the two wooden steps with deep thuds. The screen door slammed shut behind him, kicking up some dust.

Janey, although only nine, felt very strange upon hearing this. She was surprised, but not scared. She felt lucky and calm all at the same time, relaxed. She couldn't see it, but she had somehow known that the well wasn't covered, but she hadn't consciously realized it until just then, sitting at the dinner table.

This was just one of the many stories that Dave had heard growing up about his mother's psychic abilities. There were so many that after awhile, he really began to think that his mother's imagination was running away with her. Of course, Dave's father, Rick, thought that Janey was "off her rocker" with all of that "Voo-Doo energy crap." Rick always wrote off everything that happened to Janey as coincidence or some sort of strange luck. Things always had to have an explanation and nothing was ever any more than that.

Dave's thoughts about his mother's abilities changed when he also started to experience things that were unexplainable. When his life and outside occurrences began to synchronize for him, he became open to the possibility that he too might have such a power. As a young child, he had vowed to develop it and become the most powerful person in the world, of course, it was shortly after seeing the first Star Wars film; "The power is strong with this one . . ."

Dave had even tried to levitate spoons by staring at them and concentrating, always believing that if he could just get focused enough, just hit that right wavelength, it would happen. Once it finally did happen, then he would be on his way to connecting with that higher *Force*. He envisioned himself as the next Yoda, only taller and better looking, of course.

When Dave was a Junior in high school, he took a course titled, "Transpersonal Psychology." It was looked at by most of the school and all of his friends as some esoteric way to wax intellectual about "deep thoughts."

The teacher of this class taught meditation and relaxation techniques. This is no easy feat when considering that the students were hormonally charged, sugared up and caffeinated adolescents. Dave excelled in the meditations and it even made his own premonitions more prevalent and frequent. He learned that others went through what he had been experiencing and that there was even a word for it . . . *synchronicity.*

The more he meditated and gained focus, the more synchronicities he experienced and the more that he noticed little clues that life was giving him. He accepted these hints as his being able to read his own path. He was somehow tapped into the greater energy. He was beyond his mortal shell and basic existence. He was becoming some sort of free flowing being that didn't quite make sense to him and yet, it was absolutely clear in his mind. He could just see things and know things, without having to actually physically experience the event. Somehow, as weird as it was, that connection just felt right. *"Everything I see is part of me."*

There was one time that really brought it all home for him. He had been involved in a back to back meditation with a girl in his Transpersonal Psychology class. Her name was Tamika. He did not know Tamika outside of the class, and he had only seen her in the class for those first three weeks. She sat on the opposite side of the room from him. Dave hadn't even said "hi" to her.

The instructor purposely paired people together who were unfamiliar with each other. This exercise was supposed to further prove her point about the power of meditation and creative visualization to connect and shape our existence. *Thank you, Shakti Gawain.*

The students in the class sat back to back in pairs, with their respective partners. The teacher explained that the spine was a major center for energy transfer. The pairs were to close their eyes, as they were lead through a deep meditation and visualization exercise.

Dave closed his eyes and became relaxed, focused. Once the meditation had the students "in the space," the instructor asked the students to imagine walking up to his or her own house, then going through the door and looking around at everything in the immediate view. She asked that the students concentrate on every color, texture and detail. Dave did this and vividly saw the details of his own home.

Next, the instructor asked the students to picture their partner's home. They were to just try and imagine the place where the other person lived and to let the images come and go without focusing on any particular picture. The students were to take note, but not remain engaged with any image for very long. The energy had to flow, or the images would be blocked and the energy would cease to transfer the picture through the unconscious, because the conscious mind would call the person back into their own outside experience.

Dave saw an apartment door and then he went through the door and saw green carpet, blue curtains, a picture of a seascape on the wall. He had even sensed that the home felt empty and cold.

After the classroom exercise, the partners were to share what they saw of the other's home. Dave's description was so accurate that Tamika, who couldn't describe his home at all, was taken back, and a little scared. She didn't say much for the rest of the class. She was so freaked out that after class, at lunchtime, she drove Dave to her apartment. She said that her older sister, who was in college, and she lived there and that they were never home because they worked a lot in addition to school. Her older sister took care of her. They had no pets and their house *was* somewhat cold and lonely, with the aforementioned carpet, curtains and seascape painting.

As soon as they pulled up to her place, he had known exactly where he was, like a déjà-vu. Upon looking in the door, it was what he had seen in every detail. After that, Tamika and he went out for an In-N-Out burger and fries. They talked about remotely related things that eventually resolved back into the stasis of the typical high school gossip.

They were friends for the rest of the term, but not close ones, and they never really hung out much after that. She would later tell her own children about this one weird, but cool guy that had completely read her mind. Her kids, of course, would think that she was nuts.

At that adolescent point in Dave's life, he had even developed a sort of manifesto of what he thought to be "the correct belief system." It was mainly notes about energy and meditation. In one passage he had written, "God might just be the summation of all of the energy present in all living things and in the universe. It's interconnected and flowing and shaped by the thoughts, the feelings and the actions of everything. That's why God can't really be explained by any traditional form of religion; there is no complete understanding because the energy is fluid and always changing, and yet it is universal and eternal."

This made complete sense to him at the time. He thought, *if God can be everywhere at once, and see everything at once, maybe God is only the energy of everyone looking through everyone's eyes, AND, to be able to tap into that energy . . . that would be like looking through the eyes of God. And we are but pieces of that connected energy, going through physical experiences, learning lessons, on our way to a higher consciousness that revolves around connectivity, love, and understanding what it really means for everyone, and everything to be a part of 'the light' that we come from and always return to when it is time to leave the Earthbound experience of our human shells.*

Unfortunately, this way of life and way of thinking did not last very long for Dave. His seventeen year old mind and hormonal male body was trying to focus on beautiful girls and baseball; he was quite good at both. This additional heavy duty focusing on metaphysical and philosophical concerns was making him crazy and he just couldn't handle it. He felt like he was plugged in to some psychic hotline 24/7 and he didn't have control anymore. Everything he saw, it seemed, was some prelude to something else, or some form of deeper insight that he was supposed to internalize and analyze until he figured it out, just in time for something else to come up and start the whole process of the chain reactions over and over and over again.

Dave wanted to forget all of the things that kept popping into his head that were linked to something else that happened, or some other person, or even some other premonition previously experienced. They would all begin to layer upon each other until they all seemed like one unified experience. The experiences were timeless and overlapping and yet they were held within their respective timeframes. That was scary. Too scary. It was as if life was paradoxically happening everywhere, over a linear timeframe, but it all was stacked deeply to include all of the passing time at once, in one instance. So in order to stifle the visions, Dave began to smoke a lot of pot daily and he started to drink heavily on the weekends, trying to turn off or at least cloud the energy field that was constantly feeding him information.

Dave began going to parties whenever he could, and there were no shortage of those in the Bay Area. He hung around people that were mostly musicians and artists, people naturally on the fringe. *Hell, it's what every other teenager is doing.* Soon, all of the meditation vision quest was but a fading memory and any synchronicities that he had once had, or had in the future, were considered to be mere coincidences and they were dismissed immediately as such, without the briefest bit of consideration or relevance.

CHAPTER 10

About the time Dave began reading chapter 3 titled, "Who you were, Who you are and Why it Effects Who You'll Be," he fell into a deep sleep on his couch, still holding the book across his lap. The wind was soothing in his apartment, as it blew through the screen in the open window. The radio quietly hummed out George Harrison's rhythmic voice, "I really wanna see you . . . Really wanna be with you . . . Really wanna see you Lord, but it takes so long . . ."

His mind takes him through a pale gray cloud. It quickly fades away, fog running from the sun, and Dave is sitting at his desk, at work.

The patients line up. He checks in people as do the other receptionists. Dave grabs a control sheet for the examinations and then he heads away from the desk, around a corner, toward a bin that is fastened to the wall. It has several slots in which to place different examinations' paperwork. He looks down at the sheet. It reads CT, brain, so he puts it in the corresponding slot. At the moment he releases his hold of the paperwork, things start to change.

Everything appears to slow down, as if he is trudging through thick mud. People's voices blur and deepen, and Dave's eyes see the world now moving at a snail's pace. Then, as he makes his way around the corner, back towards the front desk, something snaps him back into normal speed. However, the situation has changed drastically.

The entire check in area looks like a McDonald's fast food restaurant. The receptionists all wear brown outfits, with the yellow hats, that have the letters M and I swirled into a logo on them. Their white badges all have bright red lettering that reads, "Medical Imaging Center . . . We're here to serve you!"

Dave quickly looks down at himself and he is also now in the outfit, including the matching Mc-cap. He begins to sweat profusely. The room feels like a steamy sauna. His badge begins to melt, and slowly runs down the front of his uniform, leaving drippy lines of red and white. A large neon blue sign appears on the wall that flashes several numbers across it. The numbers change rapidly. A monotonous mechanical voice bellows out, "now serving number four thousand, two hundred and ten . . . now serving number four thousand two hundred and eleven . . . now serving number four thousand, two hundred and twelve . . ."

Foam forms at the corners of Dave's mouth. His tongue shrinks away as the desert of his throat gasps for air. His heart rate quickens. He feels intense pressure building behind his eyes.

There are people yelling and pushing their way to the front of the desk. They push and climb over each other. There is a sea of wall to wall patients. People collide. Fists are thrown. There is a loud jumbled mix of men and women's voices.

"I'm next!"

"Get out of my way, Bitch!"

"Where's my service? Where's my goddamn customer satisfaction?!"

"Who the hell is working here?! Anyone?!"

"Is there a doctor in the house?!"

"I've got other things to do, you know!"

"I could frickin' die here while waiting for some moron to process my order!"

Everyone and everything is disheveled. The television set is pushed over, blowing up, sending sparks flying. Disgruntled patients throw chairs, lamps and small tables through the windows. Shattered glass falls everywhere. The radiologists sit back in their white coats, holding clip boards, hiding behind thick dark sunglasses and laughing maniacally and mechanically. The security guards stand at the doors motionless and they have steel bolts protruding from their necks that hiss with electrical charges.

Dave looks around frantically at the chaos. As the patients close in on him, he grabs his hair with both hands and screams "Noooooooo . . ."

CHAPTER 11

Kennedy awoke early and he stared at his battery powered alarm clock. It was very classic looking, like something you would see aboard and old wooden ship. He had chosen a battery clock so that there was no chance of his being late due to a power outage. Generally though, he woke up at the same time, or close to it, every morning. Even though it was Saturday with no classes for him to teach, this morning was no different. Up at 7:00am.

By 9:45am, he had showered, gotten dressed, fed Emily, and then he was on his way to the outdoor Saturday Market. The market opened at 10:00am, but Kennedy had one place to go first.

He had waited to have breakfast, as he always did on Saturdays, so that he could sit down near the window at the downtown café called Govinda's. Govinda's was a European style café that roasted their own coffee and served the best vegetarian biscuits and gravy that he had ever had, anywhere.

Kennedy glanced at the newspaper while he sipped his Sumatra coffee and waited for his breakfast. Saturdays were the only days he would even think about the news. It was as if he had some strange reading the paper ritual that had to be fulfilled, once per week. He remembered how his father had always read the paper every morning. *Gotta check the stocks*, Kennedy thought to himself.

For Kennedy, the rest of the week, outside of seeing how the San Francisco Giants were doing, was just about whatever happened to happen. He liked having this type of life. He felt that it somehow had more meaning to let things happen in life, rather than constantly being caught up in all of the sensationalized frenzies of the modern day news.

He could hear the bustle of people moving about near the market and he could see the section where the fruit and vegetable vendors were now setting up shop. Behind them, it was the courtyard stage area. That stage area, surrounded by food vendors, was where the local artists would play everything from Big Band and Dixieland Jazz to Sixties rock and roll and folk music. The music was always good, no matter what style it was.

Even further back, where he could barely see from his seat in the café, was where the clothing and other products were to be sold. It was like this every Saturday from late April until Early November. At that point in the year, the market moved inside to what was called the Holiday Market, but it just wasn't the same as the outdoor summer feeling. The market in the summer was a popular gathering place for both town residents and visitors to Eugene alike.

Soon, people would pick up a tomato, or a jar of locally grown organic jam or honey, or they might try and talk down one of the vendors on the price of a Guatemalan cotton pullover or a sterling silver bracelet.

Kennedy took a sip of his rich coffee and imagined their voices.

"Is this romaine grown locally?"

"Do you have anything in a darker blue?"

"Are these candles made of beeswax?"

"Would you go down five dollars if I bought two? Three?"

"Does anyone serve beer around here? What about wine?"

"Are you going to be here next week? Can you hold this?"

"Is this hummus made with non GMO ingredients?"

Outside the café, it was a perfect, slightly humid, partially cloudy Saturday that was nearly seventy five degrees.

When Kennedy finished his breakfast, he left the café and then he walked over to the small bandshell where a guitarist and banjo player were picking out some old Bill Monroe bluegrass tunes. He looked around and saw all of the booths, selling their wares, everything from tie dye clothing to all natural wind chimes, knitted hats for babies, crystal necklaces, precious stone earrings and African 'rain sticks' that were large pieces of a lightly colored wood and were filled with some special sort of seeds. When the big sticks were turned to an upright position, the falling seeds gave the auditory illusion of the rain falling. These instruments sold surprisingly well in a place that had no shortage of rainy sounds for most of the year.

Kennedy was enjoying the smell of all of the foods, everything from pizza to veggie burritos. Suddenly, he got a quick skunky and sweet whiff of marijuana that wafted by his face from behind him. He turned and had no idea where it had come from, as the crowds of shoppers were now becoming much larger and much more packed in. Kennedy smiled and laughed a little to himself, thinking of the times, not too long ago, that he too would sneak a fast puff or two on a Saturday morning at the market.

Kennedy turned around to see one of his coworkers from the University looking over a beaded necklace with a large amber stone on it. It was Shelley Gonzales. Shelley was a professor of Spanish and Portuguese in the Foreign Language Department. She and Kennedy used to see each other a lot, before he got his new office. The Foreign Language offices were located near the bull pen area in the Language Arts building, where Kennedy used to keep his things before becoming a full professor.

He walked up to her and said, "Maybe you should go with the amethyst instead."

Shelley turned around, answering before she saw who it was, "Excuse me . . ." Then, she figured it out and smiled. "Well, Professor Jones. Nice to see you for once."

"What do you mean by that?"

"You know, now that you are a big, tenured professor, I hardly see you any more." She laughed a little. Kennedy had always thought that she was very pretty. She was half Spanish and half Italian, with dark olive skin, long black flowing hair, and ice blue eyes.

"Wait a minute Shelley, a guy gets an office and now he's shunning you? I beg to differ. I don't see you making your way up two floors, knocking down the door to my office either." They were both hamming it up good.

"Touché, my friend. How've you been? How's your term going?"

"Pretty well, I have a couple of intro classes, you know how that goes."

"Yes, I sure do. I only have one, thank god, and the others are more advanced. I am even teaching a Romance Language History class this term."

"Sounds pretty interesting."

"So far, so good. The kids are a little slow to get going, but I think it will get better." The vendor began to look impatient, but he didn't want to lose the sale, so he kept quiet.

Kennedy thought about asking Shelley out for dinner. He had considered it before, but never let himself follow through. Just then someone bumped into him, and he turned around, but the person was gone. When Kennedy turned back to face Shelley, there was a tall, good looking Latino man leaning over Shelly's shoulder and asking her about the necklace. She spoke to him as she looked at Kennedy. "Honey, this is Kennedy Jones, oh, I mean, Doctor Kennedy Jones. We work together."

Kennedy replied jokingly, "Glad to meet you. Um, Honey is it?"

Shelley put her hand over her face and laughed a little. The rugged looking man laughed as well, and then responded in a slight accent, "My name is Julian. Pleased to meet you Doctor." They shook hands pleasantly.

"Pleased to meet you as well Julian, but Kennedy is fine." Kennedy paused for a brief moment. "Well, I guess I'll see you around campus, Dr. Gonzales." Kennedy turned to go.

She replied, "I'm sure you will. Good luck with the rest of the term." She got out her wallet to purchase the necklace from the overly patient and relieved vendor. Eugene, Oregon was a great place to live, but it was often difficult to make a living.

"Yeah, you too," Kennedy replied. He could see that Shelley was too far away and didn't hear him, and that was fine.

The rest of the day went quite well for him and it was relaxing and fairly uneventful. The skies threatened to rain more than once, but the sun always managed to peak back through and warm the few hundred people who had converged on downtown on that Saturday.

Before leaving, Kennedy purchased a Native American wall hanging that looked somewhat like a dream catcher. It was a Hopi Indian piece from a Northern California tribe that was supposed to ward off bad spirits and bring good luck to the owner. He thought, *with the weird things that have been happening lately, it's probably not a bad idea to spend the twenty bucks.*

CHAPTER 12

Monday. It was very unusual, but Kennedy was running late to his 9:00am class. He downed the last of his home brewed coffee and made a call to Dan so that he could handle the class until Kennedy could get there. He told Dan that he was about 15 minutes behind and then Kennedy asked him to take role and begin the students with the reading, The Pit and the Pendulum, by Edgar Allen Poe. Kennedy had always liked that one of Poe's stories in particular because it is one of the few where it ends on a positive note and the protagonist actually gets saved in the end.

The literature class was an intimate gathering of 20 students. They were Senior level and had had Kennedy as a professor previously, so he knew they would all give him a load of crap for being late when he finally showed up. It was a small price to pay, because after all, it was his fault.

Kennedy stepped into the room and thanked Dan quietly as Dan met him at the door. As Dan left, Kennedy walked over to his desk, sat down his briefcase and his soaked umbrella. He looked out over the students, who were reading silently. Toward the back of the room, there were two very large picture windows. It was still raining steadily outside.

Kennedy went to the board, grabbed some chalk, but was startled when he looked up to the black board. Someone had written, "A few too many brews last night, Dr. Dude?" in the brightest yellow chalk. He was surprised for a second, and then he heard the muffled laughter coming from the class. Kennedy turned around; the students were looking up smiling. He said in a joking manner, "all right, all right, I guess I had that one coming."

As the students took a couple more minutes to finish their reading, he placed a few notes on the board to begin a discussion about the Poe piece. He wrote, "Understanding" and then "Acceptance" and then "Release" on the board. He looked around and noticed that a few of the seats in the front row were empty. These were usually always filled with the

'A' students. Kennedy thought, *sometimes this cold, damp weather even gets to the best of us.*

Kennedy began to explain how the main character in the story comes to 'understand' where he is in the pit, and then how he 'accepts' the nature of his fate and situation, until he can then finally work toward his own 'release.' Fortunately, Poe had uncharacteristically allowed his character to be rescued at the last minute by an outside source. Kennedy had often wondered if Poe had actually been having a good day when he finished this particular story, as his stories, like Poe's own life, were often wrought with depression and death.

As Kennedy began to talk about how this Edgar Allen Poe story was one of the only ones that ends somewhat well, he noticed something out of place in the classroom environment. At first, it was just a soft, slowly rhythmical tapping sound, but it steadily grew louder. As he continued to lecture, his mind drifted. *What the hell is that noise? It sounds like . . . like water dripping..* He looked around and continued to speak as the dripping grew louder. He wondered, *don't they hear that?* The students seemed to be unaffected by the incessant and increasingly pervasive noise.

Drip. Pause. Drip. Pause. Drip. Pause. The noise got even louder and pounded like a heartbeat in Kennedy's mind. It began to have a direction of origin. Again, he looked about the room, telling the class about how the Spanish Inquisition was the perfect backdrop for Poe's intense story. He realized that the students could not hear it. They were oblivious to the dripping sound.

Suddenly, Kennedy felt a damp chill. It began at his feet and then it worked its way slowly up his legs. He glanced down, trying to remain nonchalant. There was a misty blue fog surrounding his feet and legs. It was creeping up to him from the front corner of the room, near the door. Again, he looked to the students. Nothing. He was on his own with this macabre occurrence. It was time to abandon the talking and get the students working independently in order to figure out what was happening to him.

Kennedy, being a very experienced and resourceful educator, said, "Okay class. Now take out a pen and paper and give me a two page analysis of the symbolism of the pendulum as it pertains to something in life. It can be the nature of being alive, or it can be time ticking away at work, etc. I'll leave it up to you. This, of course, is due at the end of class. Any questions?" Being upper classmen and most of them having had Professor Jones before, there were no questions at all. They had all learned a long time ago not to even ask how many points something was worth. The students quickly got to their work, but a few of them still grumbled quietly about having to do an impromptu write in class.

Kennedy turned around and began erasing the board, but he allowed his eyes to wander toward the door from where the fog was rolling in to him. It seeped in from under the closed door, expanding as it rose. The students worked silently and yet the fog was still there, at least for Kennedy.

Just to the right of the door, the blue became iridescent and shone bright. It quickly engulfed him in a bright flash and then subsided. But when the light returned to its original subtle glow, there was someone sitting in one of the previously empty seats in the front row. It was the seat closest to the door.

Kennedy wasn't sure who she was. She was drenched. Her hair hung in her face and she sat halfway draped over, her arms resting across the desk. She wore a white dress and was barefoot. The water dripped off of her quickly. Drip, drip, drip. It collected in a small pool that slowly expanded from under her desk, and back toward the other students. He assumed it was one of the 'A' students, maybe having walked to class after staying up too late studying. *But barefoot? In a nice white dress? In this weather?* His mind tried to reassure him that it was an 'A' student, at least at first.

"Pretty wet out there," he said to her. No response. The class worked on their papers and paid no attention. They apparently didn't hear Kennedy speaking to the woman. "Hello, miss?" He suddenly realized that she appeared unfamiliar and that she was not one of his students at all. The more he looked at her, the more he could see that she didn't look entirely normal. He began to worry that she was on heavy drugs and had just wondered in. "Are you in the right class?" Again, there was no response from anyone in the room, including this young woman now seated in the front row. It was like Kennedy had stepped behind mirrored sound proof glass and he was unable to be seen or heard. He looked at the students, but they did not respond to his talking. He raised his voice and said, "Hello out there. Anyone?" Again, there was nothing. Kennedy was becoming increasingly frightened. "Um, Miss . . ."

The young woman's left hand slowly slid off of the desk and hung at her side, swinging back and forth. Back and forth. Dripping water. Kennedy took a step toward her and the dripping water immediately stopped.

Suddenly, there was a voice. No, a whisper. "Ken-ne-dy . . . Ken-ne-dy." The female voice began to get louder. "KEN-NE-DY . . . KEN-NE-DY!"

Kennedy thought, *Oh my god, is this the same voice from the lake?! Jesus Christ! Is this that same girl? Are you kidding me? Holy shit! What is happening?!*

The students kept working, unaware of what was going on with their instructor. His adrenaline began to surge. His heartbeat quickened. Kennedy took another heavy step toward her.

The calling of his name stopped.

The young woman's head rolled across her shoulder and she slid out of the desk onto the tiled floor, hitting with a hard and squishy thud. Kennedy stepped again toward her and then he heard an ear piercing scream. It had come from outside the door.

Kennedy looked quickly toward the door and then back to the floor. The girl was gone. The seat and the desk continued to expand the pool of water with slow drips, each drop rippling out like a pebble hitting a lake. Each making a loud splashing sound as it hit.

He feverishly looked about the room; the students still in their writing coma. He thought, *where did she go? What was that scream?*

Something caught his eye, behind all of the students, out through the back windows. The girl in the white dress stood there far off in the distance, glowing that muted blue. She was facing Kennedy, the rain pouring down over her. Her right hand pointed down stiffly in front of her, and her soaked hair still completely covered her face.

She raised her extended arm, slowly, and pointed at Kennedy. His heartbeat was now in his head as well. The loud thump, thump, thump was making him insane. He thought, *me?* She nodded her head, continuing to point at him. *She just read my thoughts. What the hell is going on?!*

He screamed loudly, "What did I do?! Why won't you leave me alone?!"

She lowered her arm and cocked her hair covered face to the side. Kennedy could see in the distance that her eyes had turned jet black; vacant and lifeless. She looked as if she couldn't figure out why he didn't understand her, like something was obvious and he was just missing it.

She paused. Then, as the rain fell even harder, she gradually lifted both arms straight out to her sides, staring at Kennedy through her hair with those dark, hollow eyes. The fog quickly rolled in around her and the misty gray enveloped her until every last bit of blue essence was gone. The fog dissipated, just as quickly as it had come, leaving only the downpour. She was gone.

Kennedy stared for a second out the back window, still racing from endorphins, but utterly perplexed.

"Dr. Jones. Sir?" It was Brandon, a literature major who had transferred from Arizona State. "Hello, is there something out that window that we all need to see?"

Kennedy answered out of habit, "Excuse me?"

Brandon replied, "If we don't finish this write, since there's not much time left, can we turn this in tomorrow?"

Again, Kennedy answered blankly, "Try to get it done, but, yeah, it can be due tomorrow, as long as you keep working until the end."

Kennedy finally realized that he was back in his classroom, under more normal conditions. He looked to the desk by the front door. There was no water, no ghost and no scream coming from the other side of the door.

Another student tried to get his attention. This time it was a female Nursing major who had grown up in the San Fernando Valley. "Uh, Professor, could I like, uh, get a little help with this analysis dealy? I don't, you know, understand this whole pendulum thingy, and, um, I'm totally lost with this Poe stuff."

"The what? Oh yeah, pendulum, sure. Give me a second, I have to check on something." He walked over to his desk and pretended to go over some paperwork that was handily available on his desk. This gave him time to compose himself and to return his mind to the present situation. He walked back over to her desk and kneeled down next to her as he began to explain. "You see, the pendulum can mean many things. Some see the swaying and cutting motion as time cutting away at the years in our lives . . ."

He knew that she would probably never grasp the symbolism. Her strong points were in the well defined, literal aspects of math and science, which she was very good at. He knew this class merely filled a liberal arts requirement for her. Nevertheless, she seemed like a good kid. He would explain it as best he could, growing more relaxed and feeling more normal with every spoken word. The worst was over.

CHAPTER 13

Dave strolled through the numerous aisles of the Barnes and Noble bookstore, looking for some reading material. It had been a long time since he had gone out looking for something to read. He looked past all of the Self Help books, but figured that Christy had him covered in that department with that One More Time book.

The experience of going through this commercial bookstore seemed somewhat artificial to him. He thought, *did I just miss the boat on this whole 'one stop book, coffee and entertainment shopping experience?'*

In college, there was Black Sun Books, and although they were a good bookstore, they were very eclectic and you kind of needed to already have an idea of what you were looking for in order to be able to successfully find it there. But, it was always a great experience. Nevertheless, because of their large supply of diverse topics, Barnes and Noble was the place to go when you weren't sure what it was you needed.

He walked past the Science Fiction and then Romance, followed by the Children's section that was decked out with a large castle, fairies hanging from the ceiling and a blue stuffed dragon peering down from the corner of the room. Next to that section, just past the seating area for the Starbucks coffee kiosk, was the horror section. For some reason, this tripped his fancy. There was a large standing, cardboard facade advertising Stephen King's latest book. It showed King's face coming out of the fog and some faceless entity in rags swinging a sickle at his head with its boney hands.

Dave remembered reading King's books in high school. "Cujo," "Pet Semetery" and "The Stand" were what immediately came to mind. He remembered trying to read, "It," but it was too much for him. From the little bit that he read, he would have trouble looking at clowns or even looking down sewer drains for years to come.

There was one of King's books that caught his eye. He had heard about it, and read some reviews about it, but had never picked it up. It was, "The Gunslinger." Maybe Dave was afraid to begin something that was a part of a much larger series, seven books in all by now, and none of them very short. That seemed at the time like too long of a commitment. *What if it sucks?*

He read the back and decided that it was going to be a little different than the typical Stephen King horror book. This one appeared to be kind of like Clint Eastwood via the Spaghetti Western era meets "The Lord of the Rings." He decided that he could do that. And if he got hooked, well there were six more just waiting for him. Besides, he needed something to break up the monotony of that book that Christy had him reading. While he was actually enjoying it, it got kind of intense and it was very dry. Some fiction was definitely in order. Dave paid for the paperback, deciding that you can always get the hardcover version after deciding if the book is worthy of collecting.

As he drove home, his thought drifted back to Frances Vasquez. *Her husband died pretty young.* Dave thought about his own father, just for a minute, and then went back to thoughts of Frances. *She seemed to be taking it well, like it was all okay with her.*

It was difficult for him to understand how someone could just accept death like that. Dave thought, *she didn't seem at all resentful, like she was just happy to have had what time she had with him. She was sure that she would see him again; there was no question about it. Was it her age? Was it religion? No, it was more than that . . . something else.*

Dave wondered, *what would it be like to feel that sort of connectivity? Like you understood what it was all about. Like, where you were, where you'd been and what was to come was all one interconnected thing. How peaceful it would be to know your place and that no matter what, your choices could all make it work out correctly.*

Dave suddenly thought of something he had read in that book from Christy. It was in a chapter called, "The Passing." It had said something about when people's future lives are presented to them in the form of a vision, these visions are often morphed over a current timeframe in order for the experience to make sense, in the correct context, for the person experiencing it, at that particular time. This is how those experiences are possible to be comprehended by people in their current lifetime experience. Dave thought, *metaphysical mumbo jumbo bullshit that sells books and gives people a false sense of hope.*

He looked up and saw a bright, neon Jack in the Box clown sign. He thought, *this introspective stuff is making me hungry,* as he turned in to the parking lot for a Jumbo Jack with cheese.

That night Dave fell asleep reading his new book, "The Gunslinger." The words of Steven King echoed through his mind, even after he uncontrollably closed his eyes. "*Above, the stars were unwinking, also constant. Suns and worlds by the million. Dizzying constellations . . .*"

Dave's dreams were of him riding across the desert, alongside the main character Roland, the Gunslinger. He could feel the horse beneath him, chugging along. The sun beat down on his head and chest. He began to sweat. He could taste the stale dryness of the air.

A cave appeared in front of them; large and dark. The Gunslinger and his horse suddenly disappeared. Dave dismounted his horse and walked into the cave slowly, cautiously, and alone.

The walls begin to spin around the cave ceiling and floor. It is like looking through an empty cement mixer. Dave's now walking through the vortex. It turns downward and he slides down, down, down.

He lands on a bed. It has a worn feather comforter on it and it smells of dust. It is very cold. A young woman lies next to him, bundled in a faded knit hat and scarf. He tells her that it will be okay, that their money problems are temporary. She does not answer. A tear rolls slowly down her face as she pretends to be asleep. He whispers to her, "I love you, Charlotte."

He knows her thoughts. She wishes for more, for a better life. He knows this is the past . . . again.

Who are these people?

Why do they keep coming into my dreams?

He would swear it is him, and someone else, but how could that be? Yet, her eyes are so familiar. These green eyes are the windows to her soul.

His side of the bed collapses and he is viciously pulled from the sheet; like someone ripping a bandage from skin. He is falling again. It becomes very dark. He is cold. He curls into a ball as he falls. Naked and freezing. Fetal.

He is thrust into a bright light and lands softly on a pillow of fresh green grass. He is dressed in summer clothes and knows that he is in San Francisco, California. He hears blues music. Johnny Lee Hooker? The sun is warm and there is a light breeze blowing in off of The Bay. He sees a girl with blond hair. She turns and smiles, familiarly even though he doesn't know her. Her beautiful green eyes are flashing back the sunlight. Dave warms like honey sitting in the hot sun. A comfortable numbness rushes over him and he drifts off, deeper and even deeper . . .

There is the crash of a loud buzzer, like time running out in a high school basketball game. The sound surrounds him, gripping and pulling him away, the tearing of an old photograph, the loss of a dream. He covers his ears and winces, but it won't go away.

Dave sat up quickly and shook his head. Frustrated, he slammed his hand down on his alarm clock and it quickly died.

Part II
CONFLUENCE

"So quick bright things come to confusion."
                              —(William Shakespeare)

CHAPTER 14

Kennedy had gone to bed that night, after several glasses of wine and a few hours of some mind numbing television. He had watched something about an older male cop and a younger street wise woman attorney investigating a crime. This was followed by beautiful, halfway dressed people bouncing around in lifejackets on a perfect summer day, somewhere in Southern California. That was enough to send him into unconsciousness and eventually upstairs to his bed.

The rain showers never let up that day. They had continued to fill the drains at the curbs until the water began flooding out into the streets. And the water kept coming, there was no escaping it. Kennedy had driven through a few inches of water just to get his BMW into his driveway. For some reason, today's rain felt like it was swallowing him, like it could surround, consume, and pull him under completely.

When he had come through the door of his house earlier that evening, Emily had run and hid. She could sense that something eerily wrong had happened and she wanted nothing to do with whatever had scared Kennedy so. Now, he lay in bed, very unsure of his own sanity. Very much alone.

He said aloud, "How can this be happening? What the hell is going on?!" Emily walked by the outside of his bedroom door, peeked in for a second and then decided to continue on her way downstairs.

Kennedy turned to the window, "Well, where are you?! Goddamn it, show up! Fly through here again like you did the other night! Before . . . before you came to my classroom today! I know it was you!"

He picked up a pillow and threw it at the closed window. It missed the glass, hitting the frame. It fell to the floor and landed with a soft thud. He said, "I'm not crazy. I'm *not* goddamned nuts. Where the hell are you?!"

He put his head in his hands. "What are you trying to tell me?" He began to sob and spoke in a whisper. "What do you *want*? What do you want from *me*?" He paused and took a deep breath, trying to clear his mind. "I don't understand. Why are you doing this to me?"

Kennedy leaned back and flopped down onto the bed, staring at the ceiling. He knew that this had to be happening to him for some reason. There had to be some connection between him and this girl's ghost. He could feel it, but still did not understand it. He wondered what all of these occurrences were trying to tell him.

He looked one more time to the window, stared for a moment, took a deep breath, exhaled strongly and then closed his eyes. The rain intensified and ran a steady stream down the outside of his bedroom window. He could hear the force of the water and could almost feel the pressure of it falling all around him.

CHAPTER 15

Dave sat at work, behind his desk, watching the water run down the outside of frosted opaque windows that were across the large waiting room. It was a lull in the action; one of those strange, brief moments where you could eddy off to the side and avoid the onslaught of the day's powerful currents. For some reason, Rochelle had invited Dana, Candy and Betty out to lunch, even offered to pay. That was like adding insult to injury for Dave. Not only did he miss out on the free lunch, he had to cover the front desk by himself until they all got back.

Sometimes these breaks in the action were a curse because it allowed Dave to actually slow down and reflect on things. Not being in college any longer, he didn't have to try and sneak in some quick homework problems or read anything that had a deadline attached to it. His time was actually his, to do or think about what he chose to. That could be scary.

After getting up, making his way through the lobby and disposing of a few stray papers, gum wrappers and an empty orange plastic pill bottle, Dave sat back down. He didn't bring, "One More Time" or "The Gunslinger" with him to work because he never could have guessed that he would have any time to possibly read. The office had been teaming with patients and insurance calls and irate doctors calling tenaciously and trying to make every little hang nail into a life threatening emergency, just so they could make their one o'clock tee time.

Dave looked toward the television. Even though it was fairly large, he would often forget it was there. It was often just white noise to pacify the patients. However, today, in the vacant emptiness of the lunch hour, something caught his attention in the words flashing from the idiot box. It read, "Intelligent Design."

Dave grabbed the large remote control and flipped up the volume so that he could hear what was being said. The man stood there, white hair slicked to the side above his shining blue eyes and million dollar smile. He said that he was from the "Discovery Academy," the originators of this field of thought. *Hmmm, this actually could be interesting.*

The man on the television, Sam Christianson, began to explain, "Intelligent design is the assertion that certain features of the universe and of living things are best explained by an intelligent cause with a specific order to it, rather than an undirected process such as natural selection or evolution . . ."

This actually made some sense to Dave. He remembered reading in Christy's book about how things are not completely random and that everything in the universe works off of each other. He had thought about this stuff before, but not for a long time. Since there were still no patients, he decided to listen in for a little bit longer.

Mr. Christianson went on to say, "And of course, the magic behind the mechanism all begins with the faith in our lord, Jesus Christ."

Click.

The television quickly turned off and powered down.

Dave shouted, "What a crock of shit!" He covered his mouth and looked startled when he realized that he was still at work. Luckily, he was still alone and his slip did not offend anyone. Although he did not believe in any of it, he would not intentionally offend the believers.

Dave had previously read an article in a recent Scientific American journal that stated that, "The US National Science Teachers Association and the American Association for the Advancement of Science had termed 'Intelligent Design' as 'pseudoscience,' stating that it was based on conjecture in response to a 1987 court case and that the founders gave no hypotheses of their own." Dave knew that others had gone so far as to call it 'junk science.' He thought, *just when something starts sounding somewhat decent, they spin in the religious zealot crap and screw it all up!*

Dave sat there for a moment, feeling like he'd been tricked. He thought, *there's way more to it all than that. It's not just some imaginary, omniscient, all powerful being setting it all in motion and then threatening people with an eternity of burning in hell . . . sure, that works if you don't care to take any responsibilities for your own decisions and your own life in general.* Dave had heard it a million times before, in one version or another. "It's just God's way. He's in control and I'm just along for the ride. If I suffer enough and give enough money to the Christian cause, and try to convert more money givers, then I get to join Him in eternal peace."

Bullshit.

In reality, it has something to do with interrelations and interactions and the choices that make the course of any life what it is. Yes, choice is a big part of it. It's not just fate. Choice is what guides the fate. If people would just figure that out, and therefore make better choices that benefit all of us, the world might be a better place to live, for everyone.

Dave knew that not all Christians were bad, or even that extreme in their thoughts, but it seemed like enough of the true believers were and that it was those people who were messing things up for the rest of the world. It wasn't just the Christians though, he thought, it was any extreme interpretation of any organized religion.

Dave heard someone grabbing the handle of the office door. He realized that in his mind, he had been rehashing his basic belief system that he had come to accept back in high school. Back when he was tuned in to all the 'synchronicities' and life clues around him. Back when he thought he could actually feel the energy around him and flowing through him. Back when he could see someone else's apartment that he had never been to, during a back to back meditation. He thought, *yeah, that was long ago, in a galaxy far, far away.*

Dave greeted the elderly lady that came in through the door with a polite, "Hello" and then he went on about his business of checking her in and getting her back for her exam. She carried a large pink purse with an off white doily pattern sewn all over it. She wore a matching hat and pink gloves. It would be another hour before Rochelle and her obedient imaging disciples would return from their luncheon in order to allow him to break free for his lunch.

After the crew came back, Dave ate lunch and then finished off his day as usual. He then headed straight home to his apartment, without seeing Christy.

CHAPTER 16

Christy sat alone and stared out of the kitchen window of her townhouse, looking at the early afternoon sun as it shone golden through the branches of a large pine tree across the street. She sat down her pencil on top of her lesson planner and said, "What in the hell is wrong with him?" She was becoming increasingly frustrated with Dave's inability to overcome whatever obstacles were keeping him from being happy.

She forcefully pushed her chair back from the table and got her self a small bottle of organic apple juice from the fridge. She twisted loose the cap and took a big drink. Christy was not one to ever dwell on a situation, but she just couldn't let this go. It had been going on for far too long.

She thought, *what am I supposed to do? Just let him wallow . . . and bring me down with him?! At least he's thinking about more college . . . but . . . for what? Is that what is really going to do it for him? It seems like he's his own worst enemy and I'm lucky to even crack that shell of stone, when it comes to him discussing what is wrong with him. It's like he's a cowboy from the Old West or something. "Gotta do it alone."* The thought of Dave only wearing a cowboy hat and chaps, chewing a long piece of grass actually made her laugh and broke her tension for a moment.

The rest of the day slipped by her and she eventually was able to let go of her issues with Dave and finish her lesson planning. She thought, *yeah, summer vacation and time off my ass! If the people that complained about teachers' time off ever had to try and do the 15-hour-per-day job, for next to no pay . . . they'd think before they spoke. Oh, and then there's the constant threat of an incredible teacher being laid off by some know nothing, wannabe good ol' boy principal who is trying to get the Department Head's husband a job to replace the newly created vacancy once the good teacher is let go. Yes people, this really does happen! Let's all run out and be teachers!*

But, even with all of the extra time spent grading papers, calling parents, counseling students with problems, attending faculty, staff, and district meetings, and of course, preparing lesson units and assessments over the summer, Christy still loved her job. Teaching was what connected everything for her. It was her focal point. She knew this and had known it for a long time. She wondered how long it would take for Dave to discover that final piece to his puzzle, if it ever were to happen.

That night, Christy curled into her bed alone. Dave had suggested that he sleep at his place, because he had an early meeting the next day at work and all of the radiologists and other managing partners would be there. He knew that he couldn't be late. Christy thought that it was an excuse, but still enjoyed the idea of getting some extra sleep herself. A neighbor's white poodle barked and whined to get let back into its home (the owner's were away at a rotary function that was running late); however, Christy didn't hear the dog at all. She was finally in a deep sleep.

CHAPTER 17

That night, Dave knew that he would have to get up extra early for his meeting. The meetings with the doctors were always important, especially when the imaging center was looking for ways to downsize, even if they called it "becoming more efficient." He didn't want to be the one coming in late to that meeting and giving them cause to dismiss him. So, he went home to his apartment, had a small dinner of a boiled hot dog and a Coke and read a little from "One More Time." He was in bed by 8:00pm and fast asleep.

Dave slept restlessly. He turned from one side to another, jerking quickly. He was hot and he sweat, but he also shivered. He began to dream.

Dave gets up and walks away from his bed. His apartment begins to change and by the time he reaches his bedroom door, there are stairs going down to another level. He is now in a house, but it seems familiar to him. Even though he has no pets, a small friendly cat trots up to the edge of his door, looks at him briefly, then trots down the stairs. Dave decides to follow.

The walls of the staircase are lined with pictures, each one a scene from his life. There's one of him playing baseball. There's one of him sitting by the pool with his mother when he was in 6th Grade. There's another one of him graduating high school, then graduating college. The last picture is blank, just a frame and it makes him feel cold.

When Dave reaches the bottom of the staircase, he sees a nicely decorated room. There are beautiful sculptures, classic paintings and ironwood carvings. He can hear the faint sound of classical music, but does not recognize the composer. He sees a bottle of Cabernet wine, sitting next to the plush couch, atop a beautiful wooden coffee table. Next to the bottle, is a delicate wine glass filled half way. Dave can smell the soft scent of curry seasoning in the air.

Dave walks slowly through the house, feeling somewhat relaxed, like he belongs there. He turns past the kitchen and sees an open letter sitting atop the dining room table. The wording looks official. He heads down a hall to the bathroom. There is a large mirror hanging on the wall behind the ivory white sink. Dave approaches the sink, turns on the water to wash his hands and looks up and into the mirror.

Dave sees his own face and then it suddenly transforms into a stranger's face looking back at him. The new face is much different from his. It has a beard and shoulder length blond hair. Although Dave has never seen this person before, the eyes are his own. He realizes that this stranger's face is now his. Even though his face has completely changed, Dave knows that he is somehow still looking at himself in the mirror.

Dave quickly looks down and sees that the water from the sink is flowing over onto the floor. He frantically tries to turn off the knobs on the faucet, but the water pours out faster and faster and faster.

He looks back into the mirror and the face now has pitch black holes where the eyes were before. Dave screams as the water comes up past his waist. He turns to try and open the door, but it is locked. The water climbs quickly up to his neck and begins to creep into his mouth. He begins to choke. He looks back to the mirror, but now there is no face in it at all. The image of himself that was Kennedy is now completely gone. The reflection of Dave's face has disappeared, as if he is no longer there. There is only the reflection of the steadily rising water.

Dave sees water coming up past the bathroom window that leads outside of the house. He tries to smash the window glass with his fist, but it doesn't move. He tries the door again, but it won't open. He pulls back on the doorknob with both hands in desperation. The pressure of the water is squeezing him tightly, collapsing his lungs. He feels himself suffocating. He tries to gasp for breath, choking on cold water. The water rises and covers him completely.

Dave woke up screaming. His alarm clock was blaring and it took him a minute to realize that he was still in his apartment. He turned off the alarm, tried to catch his breath and looked at the clock. The glowing red numbers read, 8:15am.

He took a second to gather his thoughts. He leaned over and he put his sweaty head in his hands, and then he sat back up in bed. It had been a long time since he had had such an intense dream, especially a nightmare. Dave got out of bed, grabbed his clothes and headed for the kitchen for some coffee and a small breakfast. He lit a smoke and inhaled deeply, trying to steady his nerves. In the back of his mind, Dave really hoped that this dream was not trying to tell him something. It was already fading. Luckily, he still had plenty of time to get to work for the meeting.

CHAPTER 18

The meeting had gone well for him. He had made it in time and had participated as necessary, smiled at the right times and remained quiet when he needed to. He had learned long ago what proper meeting etiquette was in order to maximize visual and supportive exposure, without calling too much negative or unsupportive attention to oneself. Any against the company sentiments were to be stifled and then let out, if at all, far away from anyone who even remotely had any connection to the workplace that pays your check.

The rest of the day seemed to be a deluge of patients, coming in from both the hospital and scheduled appointments. Dave had no time to think about anything other than to grab the sign in sheet, call the names, check them in, take them back and do it all over again, with a smile, of course. All of the reception staff were working at full throttle, pedal to the metal; the customer service machine at peak performance perfection.

Dave sat down at his desk, grabbed a permanent magic marker and was about to take the list to read and cross of the next name when something caught his eye. Through the front glass, he could see that there were two orderlies from transport furiously running on either side of a metal hospital bed on wheels, coming down the hall toward the front door. The patient's face was covered with a white sheet. He had seen this a few times before. Dave knew that this was a 'stat' patient and that any delays in getting this person to the examination procedure could mean the difference between life and death. Dave dropped his pen, flew around the desk and quickly headed for the door, before the other receptionists even noticed that he had moved. Dave opened the solid door and held it back. He said earnestly, "Do you need some help?"

Neither orderly answered. Dave looked at one and then at the other. They both had the same cold steel expression of determination. They always did in this sort of situation; they were trained for emergency responsiveness. Still, they usually welcomed someone to clear the hall for them, or to get hold of the correct physician and technician. These two said absolutely nothing.

At that moment, as the bed passed him, Dave looked down at the patient. Time halted to a dead stop.

Dave is moving to get further out of the way of the patient and the transporters, but it is like trying to move through thick molasses. The voices around him sound deeper, like a 45 record played at 16. He can hardly move. His eyes drift to where the head of the patient rests beneath the sheet.

The bed is still moving, inching and the orderlies haven't stopped concentrating a bit. Everything is warped, slowed, twisted and displaced.

As his eyes focus, the edge of the sheet slowly falls away, revealing the face of a young woman. This face is someone that he is sure he has seen before, perhaps in a dream. Her eyes open quickly. They are a pure jade green. The rest of the world remains at a crawl. She slowly opens her mouth and whispers, "Ken-ne-dy. Ken-ne-dy."

Dave looks at her, confused. Then his face turns white. The image of the man's face that he saw in the mirror instantly fills his mind and he is struck with fear. He knows that other man is named Kennedy and that he and that other man are connected, are the same person.

The patient quickly bolts upright and she grabs his shirt tightly with both hands. Dave feels the pull of her grip tighten as the bed continues to creep past him, the transporters staring straight ahead blankly. She looks directly into his eyes and screams, "Daaaaavvvvviiiiiddd! Help me!"

There is a quick flash of white light and her face turns into Christy's face. Christy's eyes roll back in her head and she lets go of his shirt, dropping back. He watches Christy falling in slow motion toward the metal bed. He hears the springs recoil as she hits. She coughs out a bunch of water and it hits the floor with a splash. She is now a pale bluish color and looks like a corpse. She wears a dilapidated white

*dress beneath the sheet. The water continues to drip from her
parted lips.*

*Dave's eyes get bigger as his breath is sucked out of him.
He is overcome with the pain of losing Christy, but can't understand what is happening. He feels like he is dying, like
both Christy and he are already dead.*

The orderlies pushed past him and then time caught up
with itself. Dave could see that the patient was now not
Christy and not a woman at all, but a heavy set elderly gen-
tleman with gray hair and a greasy complexion. Dave stood
dumbfounded as he saw them rush past the desk and turn
down the hallway toward the MRI room.

Betty yelled to Dave so that he could hear her over the
busy check in room, "Dave. Dave! Are you going to get Dr.
Mitchell or what? Didn't you hear the transporters? They
need him now!" Dave stood still holding the door, with a
blank look on his face, staring back at Betty.

"I got it!" yelled Candy. Candy grabbed her front desk
phone and paged the doctor.

Dave realized that he was still at work and hurried back to
his desk. He went to grab the clip board to call a name and
thought better of it. He said, "I'm going for a minute, to, the,
uh, to lunch."

"Where are you going? We're slammed!" barked Dana.
Dave didn't even hear her. He was already going past the end
of the desk and he was headed for the break room.

He pushed though the door. There was nobody else in
the room. He reached for the phone on the wall and quickly
dialed. After a moment there was an answer. He asked,
"Christy?"

"Yes. Dave? Is that you?"

"I have to talk to you, now."

"Okay, so talk."

"No, no. Not on the phone. I'll take lunch. Meet me downstairs as soon as you can."

"But you don't usually take lunch for another . . ."

Dave interrupted, "Forget about that! Please! I'm going now. Meet me as soon as you can."

"All right. I'll leave right now, love. Are you okay?"

"I'm not totally sure, I think, I . . . I'll just see you when you get here." Dave hung up the phone, and calmly but rapidly walked out of the back door and over to the stairs. He couldn't wait for the elevator. He had to get outside immediately. He had even forgotten to punch out for lunch.

He stood outside the building, looking around for a few minutes. The day had clouded over, but there was no rain. There was a slight breeze that puffed up every few minutes, but otherwise it was calm. The coming storm had not yet arrived. Everything had appeared to return to normal again.

Christy pulled up in her newer, environmentally conscious car and Dave got in through the passenger side door. They headed for the park that was a few blocks from the hospital. Dave didn't say a word, although Christy tried to get him to talk. She gave up after a couple of tries and although she was shaken from his phone call, she figured he would say something when he was ready. She could tell that something had really gotten to him and he did not seem at all to be acting like himself.

As they sat at a bench near the river, the breeze carried the scent of cedar. They sat there quietly for a minute or two and then Dave began to speak. "Christy, I love you."

"I love you too, David. What's going on?"

"I had this dream, well nightmare, I guess."

Christy seemed a little surprised, she had expected something much more immediate, much more concrete than the lingering remnants of the previous night's upsetting dream. However, she understood that it was still on his mind to the point of leaving work for lunch early, so she asked, "Um, what happened?"

"Well, there was this emergency patient that was being wheeled in for an exam. The two transport guys were moving very quickly toward the entryway. It was busy . . ."

Christy cut in, "So, in the dream, you were at work . . ."

"Damn it, please don't patronize me!"

"I, I wasn't, I am just trying to understand. You said you had a nightmare."

"NO, that was last night. This was much worse."

"Last night you had a nightmare?"

"Jesus Christy, let me tell you what just happened today."

"Sorry, Dave. Please, please go on." Christy was surprised by Dave's combative reaction.

"Anyway, it was really busy in the office and especially in the reception room. When the patient on the bed came by me, well, I mean, I had gotten up to open the door for the orderlies and the patient." He stopped and looked at Christy, who was not about to interrupt him again. "So, just as they come by me, everything slowed down. And, well, the patient was obviously dying."

Christy decided to say, "Dave, you see this sort of thing all the time, right?"

"Not all the time, but yes, quite often. But, you don't understand. This was so *real*." Dave's heart was speeding up just thinking about the incident.

Christy was trying to be comforting and supportive. She said, "Dave, is that it?"

He replied sharply, "No, that's only the beginning."

"Tell me, then. Please."

"The sheet was over the patient's face, like when they are already dead. But, the sheet rolled back and I saw the face of a woman, a very familiar woman."

"You knew this person? Who was it? A patient that came in to the center?"

"Christy! The patient sat up and grabbed me!" Dave was getting excited and speaking more rapidly.

"Is that what scared you? What do you think it means?" Christy was trying to understand but couldn't quite get why he was being so intense.

Dave snapped again, "Christy, my god, this isn't some Freudian dream analysis shit! Please, please Love, just listen."

"Okay."

Dave tried to compose himself and then he continued. "The lady that grabbed me wasn't the patient lady anymore. It, it, it was you Christy! Christ, it was you!"

Christy's eyes got bigger and she didn't know how to react. She said, "What? I . . . I was dying?"

"No, you were already dead! You spit up some water and you were dead! You were right there on the metal bed. Then, bam! I was back at work in real time, the patient, who wasn't even a woman at all, and the orderlies were headed for the exam room. Betty was telling me to call for the doctor and I couldn't move. I was frozen in awe and disbelief." Now Dave was really worked up again.

"I was dead?" Christy got caught up in the excitement, especially thinking about Dave dreaming about her death, but, she tried to put everything back into proper perspective. "Hey, Dave. Come on, no big deal. This was only a dream, right?"

"Christy, we were both dead, even though I was standing there . . . I was dead too." Dave grabbed her hands and looked her directly in the eyes. In his most serious voice he said, "It was not a dream, I was just at work. It happened just before I called you."

"What? You were hallucinating?" Christy was really worried now. "Dave, be honest, you didn't take any weird . . ."

"No, no, no. Not hallucinating. I don't do that acid crap, you know that. I didn't make up this stuff, it wasn't like some flashback or something like that. It was real. *Very* real. I can't explain it, but it *really* did happen. But then it was, I don't know, gone."

"Maybe you're just too tired."

"Christy." He paused and put his head in his hands, then he looked back up at her, about to cry. "I'm not fucking nuts, okay?"

"I didn't say that you were, I'm just saying . . ."

"I got plenty of sleep last night. This was different, not some daytime nightmare. It was like time ripped open and something tried to tell me something. You know, like some friggin' Indian dream catcher that went haywire." He paused and saw that Christy's face was blank. "Okay, now you for sure think I'm nuts. Here's Christy, engaged to a raving goddamn lunatic!"

"No, Dave, come on, give me some credit." She was becoming calm and it actually seemed like she was trying to understand and believe him. "I love you and if you say it happened, then I believe you."

"Its kind of like some of that stuff in the book you gave me."

"You've been reading that?"

"Yes, of course. But I haven't seen anything in there like what happened to me. This is just too freaky."

Dave looked at her and into her eyes. He could see that she was not being patronizing and that she was really listening to him, trying to get it all. He calmed down a little, just a little, and said, "Christy, you were dead and I couldn't do anything about it. I felt the pain deep in my soul of not having you anymore. That was the worst of it. That was way worse than some weird time displacement, or even some crazy patient grabbing me. It was that you were gone." Dave now did start to cry a little and Christy leaned over and hugged him in close to her chest.

Christy lightly rubbed his back and said softly, "I'm not dead Baby, I'm right here."

"I know, I know. It was just *so* real. I had to see you. It *did* happen . . ." Dave took a deep breath and exhaled loudly. "You really do believe me, don't you?"

"Of course. Actually, you mentioned the book that I gave you . . ." Christy stopped, expecting some eye rolling or other form of passive aggressive resistance to her referring to that book; however, she was quite surprised to see that Dave seemed especially receptive. She continued, "That book, well it talks about these life premonition things in detail near the end."

Dave was curious, actually desperate, for some sort of explanation other than he was losing his mind. He'd listen. He asked, "Premonition things?"

"Well, that is not exactly what they call them, I think, but that is how I thought of them. The book says that sometimes, when there is about to be an event critical to your life path, or even something beyond that, strange things can come up and cross into your consciousness."

"What sort of things? Like today?"

"I'm not sure, but I would assume that today would probably qualify." She sat back and saw that Dave was listening intently. She gave him another hug and then she continued. "It says that life is always trying to clue people in to what is to come, or things that might help guide the person through the experiences to attain a higher level of enlightenment."

Dave looked at her with understanding, but deep down, he wasn't sure if he could accept it. *Is this all that Armageddon stuff that is supposed to happen in the near future?* He had been exposed to many years of the West teaching him that time is linear and then you die, and hopefully go to some amazing place forever. Such ingrained philosophy is difficult to get past. He thought back to his dream where he was someone else, *Kennedy?,* and then he was drowning in that bathroom. *Was there a connection, somehow?* Dave could not put it together and then the creeping feeling of doubt began to arise. He asked, "So this premonition thing is like a preview, or something?"

Christy was glad that Dave had settled down, but she saw that he was not totally convinced with her and the book's explanation. She answered, "Well, yeah, I guess. I'm not sure how it all works, but the book said that things are all connected and everyone and every living thing are also connected through the energy of the universe. In a sense, there is no time, but only conscious experience and learning and the sharing of energy." She stopped for a second and then continued, "I do not know if I believe all of it or even understand it. But, from what I have read in Eastern philosophy and from the book I gave you, a preview might not be the right word. I think these experiences are supposed to be more like insights to guide people, or souls, or something like that."

Dave was getting worn out. His mind was reeling and he was physically exhausted. Between the freaky inpatient ordeal and all of this metaphysical discussion, he was completely fried. He became aware of the time, the actual real time where he had to be back at work, rather than the displaced time of metaphysical unexplainable interconnected experiences. Dave said, "Christy, lets get some food. I'm going to be late."

Christy looked at her watch, more to give Dave the appropriate out that he needed than to check the time and said, "Café Yumm?"

"An excellent choice. Let's hit the drive through, okay?"

"Sure. And hey, I'll even pay." They shared a smile.

"Christy?"

"Yes, Love?"

"Thank you, for everything." He paused and then continued, "I love you."

"I love you too."

They shared a tight hug and then a soft kiss before the two of them walked back to her car, got in, and drove away from the park just as the clouds began to thicken and blanket the sky.

CHAPTER 19

Dave returned to work and the rest of the day went well, with the exception that the other receptionists were upset with him because of his leaving so suddenly. It had upset the natural order of the herd's lunch breaks. However, after his being back for an hour or so and his very focused and efficient registration work, the crew was glad to have him back and helping to weather the storm of patients. He finished out his shift and even stayed a little late just to make sure that things were in order and in tip top shape before he left.

Dave was leaving the imaging center at just a little later than his normal time, about 6:30pm. He put on his sunglasses as he walked out the employee door, just as he had done at lunch. However, the halls and the sky bridge were a completely different sight than they had been earlier. No one walked the halls. No one was there to stop and talk. No orderlies from Transport pushed patients in beds or wheelchairs. No surgeons were rushing past him to get out for a quick nicotine fix. He was the only one there.

Dave could hear a slight echo from his footsteps bouncing off of the blank tan wall as he approached the elevator. The hum of the building got even louder without the people in the halls to partially absorb it. "No crazy crowd this time" he said to himself. "It's dead in here."

The other offices had closed down at 5:30pm. Their windows were dark and their doors were locked tightly until morning. The imaging center was one of the few offices, if not the only one, that was actually open into the night in order to assist the hospital.

The sky bridge remained lit, but the hallways had cut their lighting in half. There were no longer the bright fuzzy white lights of earlier. They were now a more subdued amber yellow and they cast the silent, eerie glow of a morgue.

As he approached the elevator he looked out of the exit to the parking lot and noticed that the drizzling rain had returned. The sun had not yet set, for there was still some light, but it was now much darker. The sun and rain fought for dominance, but with the sun setting, the rain was going to win. The town of Eugene often had this type of afternoon, when the thick grey clouds and rain would suffocate the life out of the setting sun's colorful palette.

Dave got on to the empty and already open elevator, *that's weird*, and rode it to the basement where the employees had to park. The light on the elevator wall lit up, "LL2," which meant lower level two. The doors opened and he looked for his car. He saw his white 1967 VW Bug parked in the corner spot. It had a small, oval shaped orange and black San Francisco Giants sticker in the back window, next to a larger sparkly green letter "O." The car was not in bad condition, but with the exception of a CD player, it was completely stock. He'd been saving for something a little newer, something a little roomier and more useful, but he hadn't quite found that one cool vehicle in his price range. Besides, what the vehicle lacked in being cool, it made up for in cheaper gas expenses.

Dave walked over, climbed in and then he pulled out of his spot. He began driving up the two floors of the garage that would wind around and eventually lead him to the street exit.

It was nearly dark when he pulled up to the parking kiosk, flashed his blue badge at the matching blue magnetic receiving panel and watched the yellow and black striped metal crossbar lift to allow him to leave. He pulled on through and turned right onto the street. As he drove forward, he passed the little courtyard where he often enjoyed the sunshine and ate his lunch.

The rain was now coming down hard, making it difficult for him to see through the windshield. The wiper blades needed replacing and they didn't move very well anyway (inexpensive German engineering that never worked properly even when it was new.) This was no BMW.

The streetlight in front of him at Parker Avenue turned red, so he stopped. The sky bridge ran directly overhead. Parker Avenue ran left to right in front of him, between him and the hospital. He was the only car on the road.

Dave saw something move to the left and he looked out of his window, into the courtyard. There was a man with stringy long black and graying hair and a long beard to match. He wore white pants and a white lab coat. He carried a brown paper bag. Dave thought, "Oh, catching a little nip out in the rain . . . maybe hair of the dog?" But there was not booze or even wine in that bag. The man pulled a sandwich from it, dropped the bag and took a huge bite, spilling much of it onto the ground in front of him. He chewed hard like an animal and held the food in front of him with both hands as he leaned over it, seemingly to protect it. His face was still well hidden beneath all of that greasy, matted hair.

Dave thought, *how peculiar.* As Dave continued to stare at the man he thought, *what's he doing sitting out there in the rain? It's gotta be 40 degrees or less. He doesn't even have a jacket. You'd think that he'd get inside, somewhere.* At that moment, the man shot a quick look over to Dave, catching him staring. The man's face was blurry from the water running down the outside of the Volkswagen's window. Dave immediately looked back to the traffic light. *Damn . . . still red.*

Dave felt uncomfortable and wished that the stoplight would change. It seemed to be taking an unusually long time. He even thought about running it, but there were always police near the hospital and his driving record was less than perfect. A ticket was not worth it. He was already paying too much for car insurance. So, he would wait.

Dave carefully glanced back over his left shoulder toward the courtyard, trying to be inconspicuous. It was empty. He wondered, *where did that guy go?* He turned back to the light just as it turned green.

There was a loud slam on the driver's side of his Bug. Dave felt the impact that shook the entire car. He spun his head to the window and he was face to face with the greasy haired man.

The man had both hands pressed against the glass, his breath steaming the window. Dave looked at his weather soaked, frosted white face and saw that there were no eyes.

Just black, empty holes where eyes should have filled the sockets. There was no end to those holes, just paralyzing blackness. Dave was frozen. *There's . . . no . . . eyes!*

The man tilted his head sideways then smiled widely through the rancid beard, revealing a mouth half filled with teeth. Yellow, chipped and decaying teeth. The ghostly man leaned back and began to laugh hauntingly, his hands high in the air above his head, the strong wind blowing his coat backwards into the rain. *That laugh.* It was so loud. So penetrating. It was like two strong metals colliding and grinding unwillingly against each other where neither one wins. The psychotic laugh sent chills through Dave's body. He screamed, "I'm fuck-ing out-ta here!"

Dave punched the gas pedal to the floorboards and the rear wheels spun in the rain, then gripped and sent him flying into the intersection. He cranked the steering wheel to the left to make the turn onto the one way just in time before colliding with the sidewalk in front of the hospital. Dave sped away down Parker Avenue. He heard the laughter begin to fade. He looked in the rearview mirror to see that the man was fading into the rain. And then he was gone.

Dave drove as fast as he could. He drove far away. Far from the imaging center. Far from the courtyard. Far from the laughing eyeless corpse in white.

Upon arriving at his apartment, Dave rushed right in. He didn't look back. He went inside, locked the door and immediately turned on the TV. Sometimes, mind numbing commercials can wear away the intensity of a situation. Dave didn't call Christy this time. Whatever was going on was something that he needed to figure out on his own without involving her. Besides, dumping interdimensional psycho babble onto your loved one should only be done once per day, at the most.

It took awhile and after spending the first hour at home jumping at every little noise and repeatedly checking the window, he settled down to the point where he felt fairly secure that nothing else was going to happen. He also resigned himself to the idea that if it did happen, then he'd just have to deal with it and there wasn't too much that he could do about it.

The television had gotten really boring. The only things on were crime detective shows or infomercials selling cheap looking jewelry. He clicked the TV off.

It was getting late, but Dave was not ready to go to sleep. He saw the "One More Time" book sitting on the coffee table and decided it might be a good idea to do a little research.

He flipped to the table of contents and saw a section called, "Realignment" that had the subheading of "when a life is out of whack and things seem unfamiliar." Dave thought, *unfamiliar is an understatement!* He turned to page 42 where that section began.

From what he could gather in the chapter, he needed to change things up and judging by the experiences or whatever they were that he was having, the changes would need to be pretty extreme and needed to happen pretty damn soon. He thought, *okay, no more procrastination. I am not going to sit here and wallow in self pity.* Dave decided that he would pursue the PhD program and reconnect with that time in his life where he felt successful and when the future for him was bright.

CHAPTER 20

The next morning, Dave woke up extra early and called in sick to work. He wasn't scheduled to meet with Christy for lunch, so he didn't bother calling her. He hoped that she wouldn't take it wrong, but he needed to be in his own space. He would call her later in the day. He knew that she was probably worried about him, but he also knew that she trusted his judgments and would always understand. He thought, *she really is the right one.*

After having some coffee and a cigarette, he got dressed and jumped into the VW. It didn't start. Dave got out, opened the rear hatch, messed around with some wires, closed the hatch and got back into the car. After some trying, the car finally started. Dave was getting tired of dealing with the hit and miss reliability of the Volkswagen.

He drove to the campus of the University of Oregon. Dave parked, paid the meter for three hours and began walking across campus toward the Journalism School where he had spent so much time during his undergraduate degree program.

He approached the door and saw that the over one hundred year old school was going to be having some renovations done to update the Chambers Electronic Media Center (CEMC) and improve the facilities. Dave was curious as to what new equipment would be brought in. He also wanted to know if all of his old professors were still there, since he'd been out of the loop for a few years now. In particular, he wanted to see Dr. Upton. James Upton was a former broadcaster in the national news for over twenty years before changing careers into teaching. He had won several Emmy's and other awards for his reporting and for his humanitarian efforts. Dr. Upton was a good guy and Dave's former advisor.

When Dave was attending the university as an undergraduate student, Dr. Upton had sort of adopted him. He saw Dave's maturity and his incredible potential as a journalist, so he made available to him opportunities and responsibilities that other students did not get. Dave was a Technology Monitor, which meant that he would actually teach a lab class once per week for Dr. Upton. Also, Dave would assist other students with the equipment, setting up projects and the editing of filmed sequences. Basically, Dave was a teaching assistant, but while he was still an undergraduate student.

This status as a Tech Monitor afforded him luxuries within the department as well. Although the Graduate Journalism and Communications Program at the University of Oregon was extremely competitive for admissions, Dave had worked his way into a position where he was valued and, at least at that time, could have rolled right into the graduate degree and bypassed all of the competition. Of course, his grades were top notch as well, so it was not like he wouldn't have deserved admission anyway.

Dave walked into those hallowed halls that housed the "J School." He walked down the long hallway that normally held pictures of successful news and film media people hanging on the wall, especially highlighting the U of O success stories such as the author of "Fight Club," Chuck Palahniuk, who was in the graduating class of 1986. But now, the walls were blank and mostly covered with thick, clear plastic due to all of the construction dust. Classes had been temporarily moved from the CEMC to the English Department's Film section across campus.

Dave walked into the office. Patricia Woodman sat behind the desk, where she had sat for several years, addressing the needs of Journalism School staff and students alike. She immediately recognized Dave and said, "Well, Mr. Jones. How the heck are you?"

Dave felt reassured that he had received such a welcome, especially after having been gone for so long. He answered, "Pretty good Patti, and you?"

"Oh, I'm fine." She then leaned over the counter to play at a whisper, "I wish the damn construction would finish up, though." She smiled and sat back in her chair. "So, what brings you in here?"

"Well, I would like to pick up some information on the PhD program." *That felt good. It felt right, just to say that . . . to make that first step. Wow! Could that cheesy looking reincarnation book be right?*

"Okay, give me a second and I can put a packet together for you." She stood up and began shuffling some papers around. "You know that it is too late for this year, right?"

"Yeah, of course. This is for next year, unless there are midyear admissions?" Dave said this more hoping than expecting.

As Patricia finished up the packet and handed it to him she said, "Unfortunately Mr. Jones, even for you there are only once per year admissions. With so many highly qualified candidates applying, it has become very competitive."

Dave got a little apprehensive, although that was not Patricia's intent. "So, do you think I have a chance for next year's entrance?"

"Do you have a good topic for research?"

"I'm thinking about doing multicultural representations from the inception of American film to present day, and analyzing how things changed and how they reflected the sociopolitical environment of given timeframes throughout history, or something close to that." Dave had actually thought this one out ahead of time, and it was one of Dr. Upton's specialties.

Patricia took in what he said then replied, "sounds like Dr. Upton would be your advisor?"

Dave laughed a little, "Yes. I was hoping so. Is he around?"

"I think he's upstairs. Head on up." She turned around, then back. "Oh yeah, I think that since you can pair your dissertation topic up so well with someone in the department, I think you have an excellent shot at admissions, especially if you are planning on working in the CEMC again, or tutoring undergraduate students."

"I'll do whatever is needed," he replied.

"You always do, David. Take care." She smiled and went back to pursuing her work.

Dave said, "I'll see you around, hopefully more often." He walked out of the office and over to the elevator. He rode it to the third floor and then headed down the hall towards Dr. Upton's office.

When he reached the office, he saw that the door was open. There, in the back near the window sat Dr. Upton. Without even looking up he said, "Mr. Jones. I have not had a good Technology Monitor since you graduated." Then he smiled, stood up and walked over to meet Dave at the door. They shook hands and then Dr. Upton invited him in to sit down, as he gave Dave a fatherly pat on the back.

Dr. Upton was fairly tall and now he wore his hair longer than when he was reporting the news. His hair was grey and fading black, as was his well trimmed moustache. He remained in good shape through swimming every morning. He asked Dave, "so, what brings you here? Are you feeling prodigal?"

"Well, Dr. Upton . . ."

Dr. Upton cut in, "David, please call me James. You've already graduated."

The two of them talked for close to an hour, discussing the program requirements and just doing some general catching up. It felt good. Dave was returning to his element and things seemed to just be rolling forward. Dr. Upton discussed a book project that he might be able to get Dave into working on, as well as his reassuring Dave that he would be able to make admissions for the following year and be accepted into the PhD program. Dr. Upton also explained that if Dave's student teaching went well, required of all PhD candidates, that there was a chance that he could be picked up at the end of the PhD program as an adjunct professor. Dr. Upton had been making plans to retire in the next three to four years and with Dave's research topic for his dissertation being very similar to Dr. Upton's research, it would seem like a natural match to bring him on board as a replacement. However, as Upton explained, it was all speculative at that point.

Dave was excited. It seemed that so many doors were now opening; so many road signs pointing the way to a satisfying and happy future. As the two of them finished up their conversations, they exchanged personal emails. Dr. Upton told Dave to keep in touch and to let him know when he had filed all of the paperwork for the following year's admission to the program. Dave promised that he would and then they said good bye.

On the way home, Dave was feeling elated. He had completely forgotten about the menacing experiences from the previous day. He drove downtown, stopped in to Bagelsphere and had a toasted turkey and cream cheese bagel with cranberry. It was delicious. He sat outside at a small metal table and thought about his new life that was unfolding and how it seemed so right. The sun had come out and although the day was not overly warm, it was very comfortable.

After finishing his lunch, Dave was driving home and saw a used car dealership. He thought, *maybe I'll just look.* That was all it took. Within an hour he had traded in the failing VW and purchased and older pick up truck. It needed some cosmetic work, but ran strongly and had both a CD player and air conditioning. The monthly payment was very small and would not break him either. Dave thought, *a new vehicle for a new life.*

Dave called Christy from a pay phone to tell her the news about his taking the day off and buying the truck. She seemed pretty neutral about the whole thing, but she knew that Dave had been thinking about trading in the bug for something a little bigger and more reliable. She was surprised that he got an older truck, supposing that he would go the more environmentally friendly route that she had gone with her car. But, *to each their own*, she thought. She was just glad that his morning had gone well and that there was no new craziness to report.

Christy sensed that there was something else. She said, "Are you okay? Is there anything else going on?"

"Well, I can tell you about that later. Don't worry, there hasn't been any scary monsters or anything like that."

"Uh, okay, good. What do you have planned?"

"Well, it *is* Friday. How about we go to New Plymouth for the weekend?"

"Really? That sounds great! What time can you pick me up?"

"Before we get too excited, is the cabin available?" Dave realized that he had forgotten to check. The cabin was shared between Christy and another girl, Michelle. They had bought it together really cheap while they were still in college. New Plymouth was a drive and the recreation of the area had not yet caught on, so the price was affordable for the two girls.

"Yeah, yeah, Michelle is in Europe for a month."

"Must be nice."

"You know Michelle, her rich parents pay for a lot of trips." Christy and Dave both laughed. Then she followed up with, "Your right . . . must be nice."

Dave said, "cool. Okay, let me go home and get my stuff together. I have to run some paperwork by the DMV also. So, I'll be over, uh, say, early evening?" He knew that this sounded vague, but it was the best he could do at that moment.

"Sure. I'll be ready by five or six and then just hang out. Do what you gotta do." Christy remembered something and spoke suddenly, "Oh, my car is in the shop for the shocks. Can we take this new vehicle of yours to the cabin?"

"Sure."

"Okay. I'll go pack a bag."

"See you soon in the new rig. I love you."

"I love you too, baby. See you in a little bit."

Christy knew that something felt different; something felt good. She could sense that Dave was in very good spirits and that was something that she had not seen in a long time. She sensed his new feelings of confidence in the future. She thought, *maybe the tide is changing.*

Dave hurried home after his errands and put together a bag for the weekend. At this time of year, the Western Oregon weather was very unpredictable and many people often got caught in the cold or in a downpour. He grabbed clothes for all seasons ranging from shorts and t shirts to jeans, wool socks, a thick Levi denim jacket and a knit beanie. Of course, he also packed rain gear. Then, he got into his truck and headed over to Christy's house.

CHAPTER 21

On the way over to Christy's house, Dave was feeling particularly in stasis. He decided that it was time for the date to be set. This weekend, he was going to ask Christy to set a definite wedding date while they were at the cabin in New Plymouth. The cabin was the perfect place, since it was where they had taken their first out of town excursion as a couple, a few years prior. Dave wouldn't bring up the wedding plans until they got to New Plymouth and got unpacked. Then, over a bottle of wine, he'd open up the topic. He'd also decided that he would get rid of his apartment and move in with Christy, something that she had been strongly suggesting for quite some time. Her place was nice and it would do, at least until they could buy a house that might be big enough for the two of them to think about starting to have kids.

Dave knew that Christy would be surprised, elated and relieved all at the same time. Christy had waited patiently for a long time for this wedding to come about. Although she had voiced her concern and disapproval of Dave's postponement of the wedding for some 'better time in the future,' for whatever reason, she had mostly been quiet about the whole thing, assuming that Dave would eventually get his head together and come around. It appeared that something had clicked for him and it finally was that time.

Dave's life plan was becoming increasingly clearer by the minute, like he had stepped in and created a lucid dream that would carry him wherever he desired to go. In his mind, all it took was making that first effort. He had just needed to put the ball in play and wait for the positive results, the synchronicities. It felt good to not feel trapped and to even just have the possibility of something working out in his favor. Dave had begun to feel that he was back on the right path and actually making things happen, instead of reacting to whatever life threw at him. His energy was reconnected and flowing strongly through him again.

The drive over from his apartment was comforting in his recently purchased truck. He drove down the streets of Eugene, the red and primered truck humming along. Dave felt a sense of nostalgia for the older truck, like he was at peace in a time long forgotten. He played the radio on a local oldies station. He hummed along as the music played soulfully and the voices sang out the popular Motown hit by the Three Degrees, "When Will I See You Again?"

When Dave arrived at her apartment, Christy was sitting near the window, in an older wooden rocking chair. She had told him the story before of how she saw that chair in the thrift store window and kept thinking about it as she drove home. She didn't know why, but she couldn't let it go, like it was already hers and she had no choice in the matter.

She had gone back to the Goodwill early the next day and picked it up. The chair had been sitting there for awhile before the store clerks decided to move it up to the window and mark down the price. It had needed some sanding and a new coat of varnish to bring it back again, but it was a very old antique from the 1930's and well worth restoring. With a little time and effort, the chair seemed to almost glow with renewal. Christy had a knack for helping things usher in a new life.

Dave waited in the truck, while Christy grabbed her bag and her raincoat and gloves. Although the day had been somewhat sunny and warmer, the weather had since turned unexpectedly cold and the rain was coming down steadily. The meteorologists had predicted that later that night there would be slush turning to snow as the elevations increased in the mountainous areas outside of town.

The trip from Eugene to New Plymouth would take them over the mountains and past Canyon Lake. The drive was a few hours in the best of conditions and it was already nearing sunset. Dave was glad that he now had the truck; the Volkswagen Bug couldn't do too much in adverse weather and the heater on it was pretty much nonexistent due to the tiny air cooled engine that powered the VW. The truck was much more powerful, comfortable and the heater in it worked very well.

The truck rolled to a stop in front of Christy's place. Christy came out of her place, locked the door and then flipped her jacket hood over her head. Her jacket covered the beautiful light, white sun dress that seemed so appropriate earlier in the day. She now moved quickly to get into the truck and avoid the elements. Dave grabbed the column shifter and shifted the automatic transmission into drive.

Christy said, "Hey, nice truck! Does this thing have a heater?" She chuckled, thinking of the cold experiences in the former Volkswagen Bug.

Dave said jokingly, "Hey, don't make fun of my new ride."

Christy said, "No really, I'm freezing in this dress!"

"But you look, hot!" Dave smiled and Christy gave a smile back.

Dave turned the heater to high. "You'll be begging me to turn it off in a few minutes," he said as he laughed.

"I hope so. I wish my car wasn't in the shop."

"Yeah, but you don't like to drive at night, anyway. Besides, we need to break this thing in."

Christy said, "Well, I would have just made you drive anyway," and then she chuckled.

"Probably right," he said as he laughed.

After another minute or so, Christy said, "Okay, you can turn it down now. That thing really puts out the heat."

"These older trucks are like that. It has a V8 and they run pretty warm." Christy knew what a V8 engine was from all of the time being around Dave. He was no mechanic, but he could troubleshoot and fix most any small repair. Her car had been in need of shocks and Dave had figured that it was better to have a professional install them, someone with the correct tools, who would warranty the work. As Dave had gotten older, he had realized that saving money was great but a lifetime warranty with a replacement clause couldn't be beat.

As the truck moved along, Christy and Dave talked about miscellaneous things ranging from her school teaching and how it had been going recently, to Dave's frustration with his job. Christy was ready to hear the same old, 'I keep getting screwed by life' pity party from Dave, but this time was different, she could sense it. He seemed more confident and less cynical, understanding that he would not be at the imaging center forever, even though it had seemed like it.

Dave pointed to the middle of the truck's black leather bench seat and said, "Hey, take a look under that CD. Look at the paperwork." To Christy, Dave seemed very proud of whatever it was that he was going to show her.

Christy asked as she picked up the CD and looked at the cover, "Jim Croce, huh? What is this about?"

Dave replied, "You know, the 70s. Kickin' it old school, yo." Christy rolled her eyes at Dave trying to be soulful. Dave smiled at her expression and then explained, "It just seemed like good travel music. Hey, never mind that. Look at the paperwork, not the music."

Christy picked up the application and information sheet. She put the CD back on the seat between them. She read the forms over, while Dave smirked.

"David Jones, are you serious? Wow! When would this all start?"

"Well, it did start when I went in today and discussed my thesis topic with . . ."

"Doctor Upton?" She interjected.

"Yes. *James* told me that I have a good shot at getting in and maybe someday even rolling it into an adjunct professorship. The PhD program only starts in the Fall term. I spoke to Patricia the department administrative assistant this morning and she said they could work it out. She totally remembered me, too. Cool, huh?" Dave sounded excited and his positive energy was catching on to Christy as well.

"Are you sure this is what you want?" Christy deep down knew that this is what he had wanted ever since graduating with his Bachelor's degree, but she also wanted to make sure that this wasn't some sort of bipolar, on the bandwagon for now type of idea.

"Well, I'm about tired of working in a McRadiate building. And, more than likely they are going to give me a schol-
arship or some other forms of tuition assistance, if I agree to
teach. Of course I'd do that."

"Dave, this seems so great for you, for us, for our future."

Dave replied, "So, as long as you don't mind being married to a student for awhile." He paused because that had sort
of slipped out. He continued, "I think we should talk about
setting a definitive get married date when we get to New
Plymouth." Dave couldn't wait until reaching the cabin, the
timing was too right to not say something.

Christy's eyes bugged; she hadn't expected that at all.
"And, does that mean what I think it does?"

Dave smiled and glanced at her for a quick second before
refocusing on the road. He said, "I'll have to give 30 days at
my place, but can you cut me a break on the rent for a few
months?"

Christy laughed and threw her arms around Dave and
kissed his cheek. "I love you, Mr. David Jones."

"I love you too. I've always known that you're the one."
When he said that, the words seemed to especially resonate
within his soul. He kissed her on the cheek and she snuggled
in close to him as the last bit of sun faded from the sky and
was blotted out by a thick cloud.

PART III

AWAKENING

"And when you hear that song, come crying like the wind, it seems like all this life was just a dream."
—Robert Hunter

CHAPTER 22

The two had been traveling for a few hours and the storm had intensified as they climbed up the steep mountain road. Christy had fallen in and out of sleep lying pressed up against Dave's shoulder. She was unaware that the weather had changed so drastically. Dave remained cool behind the wheel, but he was having a little more trouble now that the road was snaking in a much more sinuous manner. The pitch engulfed and swallowed everything outside of the limited view of the headlights. The wind gusted hard and the truck tried to sway, but Dave kept a tight grip on the wheel, staying focused on the road.

The rain came down in icy sheets and covered the crooked mountain road in a few inches of water. The ebony night sky held no moon behind the dense cloud cover. There was only rain and blackness.

The older red pick up truck made its way along the road, its dim headlights wincing and struggling through the downpour. The truck picked up speed as it crossed the crest of the highest peak and headed downward from the summit. Downward towards Canyon Lake, some nine to twelve hundred feet below. Small patches of dirty white slush reflected back from the cliff side of the road, off to the right, fuzzy in the vehicle's muted light.

After several minutes of silence, Christy began to speak. She said, "This is the storm that the news has been warning us about for over a week. I thought it wouldn't hit hard until tomorrow, or even the next day."

Dave said, "Yeah, I heard the same thing. Kinda weird, but it happens." He acted like he wasn't concerned, but he had driven this road before in this type of storm and he was a little antsy inside to be over the mountain and to get closer to New Plymouth where the roads ran fairly straight. However, he remained cool in front of Christy. Dave continued, "well, there's no turning back now, we're on our way. We'll be there soon after we come down off of this mountain."

Christy replied, "Yeah, this weather might add a little time, but we'll still get there in plenty of time to kick back and enjoy ourselves." She added, "We can start working on our new life together."

Dave tried to think of something that would break up the monotony of the rain soaked, wind whipped drive. "Maybe we should listen to some music, to lighten up this travel time." He paused, and then continued, "Hey, you should grab that CD off of the seat and throw it in to the player."

Christy opened the plastic case and pushed the CD in to the player. Jim Croce began to play the first few chords of "Time in a Bottle." The song seemed to cry out in the night like the wind that blew hard against the truck and made the steering wheel hard to control. An 'om' like resonance from the song pierced threw them at that moment; they both felt it. It was a split second of existential clarity and connectivity that felt like the warm summer sun.

There was movement to the side of the road as the truck approached a sweeping corner. Dave, driving intently and focusing only on what was directly in front of him, had missed it. The movement caught the passenger's attention. Christy shouted, "Look out!"

Something darted in front of the truck; it was a fast blur in the heavy rain. Dave's heart raced and his breaths came in quick pants. Christy's eyes were wide open as she forcefully grabbed the passenger door's arm and held it with all her might.

A large white bird flew in front of the headlights. As it did, it cocked its head to the side and stared at them through the icy and soaked windshield, and then it disappeared into the night as it let out a shrill and deafening wail. The eyes of the white ibis were jet black and hollow.

The truck brakes squealed through the constant sound of heavy water pounding the road. The back wheels broke free. The truck slid quickly across the road as the two of them sped towards the guardrail.

They hit it head on and crashed hard through the thick steel and wood, with a sound like the snapping of dry bones, tearing loose several support beams and twisting the steel bumper of the truck. The impact was tremendous and threw both of them, even with their seat belts fastened. It echoed throughout the canyon. Both of them were thrown forward very hard when the truck hit.

The truck shot out over the side of the tall hill and dove headfirst downward, its lights shining through the foggy rain and casting a dim glow over the lake. This time, Dave saw no flash of light sending him into the illusion of another life experience. He was now back in real time, for better or for worse, in his current real life experience.

As the truck fell, Christy was silent. Dave looked over and began to tell her to brace herself for the impact with the lake. It was too late.

Christy was hunched over the smashed dashboard, her eyes completely shut. Her seatbelt had come unlatched. Blood was pouring from her shattered nose and mouth. She was dead.

Dave leaned over and held onto her as much as his tourniquet seatbelt would allow. He kissed the back of her head; he could smell her soft, fresh hair. His eyes began to stream. Dave's scream was a banshee cry piercing the cold wet air, "NOOOOOOOOOO!"

As the truck fell more rapidly, the headlights shone brighter and brighter, illuminating a large pale gold circle near the center of the deep canyon lake. The rain glistened through the headlights' beams and lit up the night.

The truck smacked the water with such force that it immediately sank. Dave felt it hit and his head was whipped forward into the steering column. He was in great pain, but he was still alive.

He caught a glimpse of himself in the rearview mirror; blood now ran from a large slice across his forehead. Dave looked again to Christy, realizing there was nothing that he could do.

He tried furiously to unbuckle his belt. He fought with it, but it wouldn't give. He searched for something to cut the belt with, looking to the floor, the seat and to the twisted open glove box. Nothing. The pressure from the water grew stronger and the windows began to bow. For a brief instant, he thought of his previous nightmare of him in the bathroom, with all of that water and that other man's face looking back at him from within the mirror. Dave was running out of time.

The truck had rotated under the water as it continued to sink, a little slower and at that point the truck bed sank first. The front of the truck pointed upward, toward the surface. Dave could see his headlights hitting the top of the water from beneath the surface. Heavy raindrops splashed small ripples into the light from above, as he sank deeper and deeper into the abyss.

Dave screamed in anger, "this isn't fair!" and he smashed his fists against the steering wheel. "Why now? Why like *this*?" He wouldn't accept that this was it for him . . . for them. He shouted, "This is bullshit! I was just getting my life together!"

The top of the water and the raindrop ripples disappeared from sight. The headlights only shined dimly through the deep water.

Dave looked to Christy with cheeks covered with tears and said, "All I really wanted was a chance to make it right." He sobbed. "I meant to tell you that, that, that I feel like we've been through this before, but it wasn't ever quite right. I'm sorry. I'm so goddamned sorry, Christy." He took a deep breath. "Goddamn, this is really it."

Dave leaned over and lightly ran his fingers through her blood stained hair. He could feel that he was running out of air in the cab of the truck. The water began to come in through the vents, slowly at first and then more rapidly. He closed his eyes and was lost in his own mind. Although the CD player had long since ceased, Jim Croce's lyrics filled his head . . ."*If I could put time in a bottle, the first thing that I'd like to do . . . is to save everyday, until eternity passes away, just to spend them with you . . .*"

CHAPTER 23

After her scream and the initial shock, Christy saw the guardrail coming upon them quickly. She should have been terrified. But, for some reason it didn't upset her. It didn't even surprise her. It was almost like she had expected it. Just before impact, her muscles began to relax and she suddenly felt at peace. Her mind slowed and she felt herself getting lighter, floating like a feather. After that transitional moment, it got very quiet and she seemed to be viewing everything from above her own body. It was like it wasn't her body at all anymore and her spirit was free to do something else now.

Suddenly, there was a bright flash of white light in her mind and then in that split second, it all made sense.

Christy's mind was saturated with images, thoughts, sounds, smells, and sensational feelings. One would lead to the next, and the next, and the next. They seemed to play out in order like a slide show, but also all at the same time. The incarnations of many lives were simultaneous and connected and yet they were each individual occurrences. There were infinite scenes with meticulously precise descriptions. Her mind immediately absorbed and processed everything.

She is a child.

She runs through the large back yard, her pigtails dancing about. She climbs onto a rope swing that her father has made with an old tire. She sits on the swing and gently rocks back and forth, back and forth. The sun is warm. She remembers how simple everything was; how the days just came and went and each one held a new adventure. She looks out over the yard and takes a deep breath laden with roses and honeysuckles.

The sky clouds over and the dry crack of loud thunder snaps the air.

She is now in a dried out field, running for her house, fearing the coming windstorm that will blow dust in the air for miles. She remembers that the last time this happened, it was hard to breath for several days and that the sky was black with dust.

This house she knows is hers. The house is very old and worn. The paint is chipped and the roof is missing shingles. The dust sits thick across the busted up wooden porch. One window is covered with newspaper because it has been broken. She somehow knows this is a farm in Oklahoma.

Now, she is in her early twenties. She feels different, like it is her, but only in a distant memory. She carries a bucket of water from the well and runs past a rusted and dead Model 'A' Ford.

She bursts through the front door and sets the bucket down on the floor. She slams the door, turns the lock, runs and pulls the shades down over the windows and waits for the storm. She begins to cry as she collapses on the old couch from exhaustion and hunger. She thinks, "I can't take this. He has to do something else . . . I, I can't do this anymore . . ."

She jumps to a different day, like turning the page in a book. She's with a handsome man who has on greasy coveralls; his knuckles are chafed and he has blisters on the palms of his hands. He holds a cigarette in one hand and a wrench in the other.

She's telling him that it's his fault they can't pay the rent and it's a good thing that they don't have any kids. She doesn't recognize him, but knows his name. She yells, "You used to have drive, you were going to be someone! I was going to be someone! But now, look at this dive we live in." *She steps closer to him.* "What are you waiting for, for life to hand you a goddamn royal flush?!"

He yells, "You *were the one that said, 'A farm could be fun . . . a good way to make a living! If you weren't such a gold digger, we'd be a whole lot better off. You're never satisfied! This farm is a goddamned dust bowl! I had to take another job as a mechanic. I hate working on cars!"* *He slams the wrench down on the kitchen table and takes a deep drag of his smoke.* "You wouldn't move to California when I asked *you to, and now we're screwed!* You *keep putting off having kids!* You *think 'if only someday we have enough money.' Shit, we had enough money before we got this godforsaken farmland!"*

She knows he's right, but will not admit it . . . she'd rather die first.

"You've never had the drive to figure anything out on your own. You never have known what you wanted to do." She glares at him with an evil look and continues, "You better figure it out and get us the hell out of here you son of a . . ."

Her cursing response becomes muffled and distant. She thinks that they should've made it as a couple. Something should have been different. If either one of them could have just seen it. They were destined to be happy together.

He is the right one for her. But, the timing is off or something. They're not quite the right people . . . yet? She sees the two fighting in divorce court, but she can feel in her heart that somehow it's not over.

The man fades away. The walls of the farmhouse melt and run into a big puddle. The puddle slowly turns into a rain puddle. It reflects the many shades of gray that fill the sky. Little drops of rain hit it, splashing up tiny waves that eventually ripple out.

The puddle becomes a small part of a much larger picture. Christy sees herself walking to class at the University of Oregon, holding an umbrella. She walks down a long hallway and then through an open classroom door.

Instantly she is transported to a large high end clothing store. Outside the store window, the weather is typical of winter on the East Coast; brown and slushy snow sits in the gutter, just off of the sidewalk. Well dressed people in heavy wool coats and hats hold lattes and talk on cell phones, their breaths turning to icy fog as it leaves their mouths.

She looks in the full length mirror of her dressing room and sees her hair is done up with lots of hairspray. The sign above the mirror says, "Saks 5th Avenue." She is wearing a great deal of makeup and shiny diamond jewelry hangs *around her neck, her ears and her wrists. She smells the perfume and thinks,* Claiborne? No wait, it's Chanel No.5.

She looks at her outfit, a black power suit that makes her the badass at any business meeting. She is impressed by the look of the suit, but is not overly content with her life. She feels hollow and that it is all so temporary. She leaves the dressing room, pays the clerk in cash and walks out the glass sliding door of the store.

The temperature changes from chilly and damp to warm and crisp. She finds herself on the sun soaked sand of a Pacific Ocean beach.

It is California in the summer. She has left the East coast and her materialistic life to rejoin the one she loved before she left for college. She turns to see a white BMW pull up beside her. She opens the door and climbs in. She sits next to a handsome man, but cannot completely see his face. He has shoulder length blond hair and glasses. He is a university professor in Oregon who is on vacation. They love each other. She knows his name is Kennedy. She knows that somehow, somewhere, that he is really Dave and that her name will be Ashley in this next world.

Her sunglasses reflect the sun as she brushes her long blond hair from her face. She looks out of the passenger window to see a boy. He walks with his shirt off, his long hair blowing in the breeze. She smiles at the boy as he looks up to see her.

The day quickly fades, the ocean air becomes just a faint memory of that sweet salty scent. The images begin to come at her more rapidly, from every direction. They are a rolodex of images, gaining speed until it is all a blur . . .

Suddenly, it is clear again. There is but one thought in her mind now. She sees herself riding in the truck with Dave, earlier that day, when he had talked about going back to school. She sees the informational papers sitting on the bench seat. She sees the Jim Croce CD on top of the papers. She watches herself reach for it.

CHAPTER 24

Dave's mind began to wander. The truck's lights fizzled and were gone. It was completely black.

He heard a voice in the distance calling his name, "Dav-id . . . Dav-id . . ." He recognized the voice as being that of Christy, but at the same time, it wasn't. The voice had a phantasmagorical echo, like someone was running it through an old Fender tube amplifier with a lot of eerie reverb. It continued. "Dav-id . . . Dav-id . . . DAAAAVVVVE."

He opened his eyes and for a second he thought he saw Christy outside and in front of the truck, floating in the water. Something was different about her, though. She had changed. She was the figure of her beautiful self, but nearly transparent and outlined in a blue aura that shined around her. Somewhere in the back of his mind, Dave knew he had seen this phantasm a few times before, but not when he was himself, when he was Kennedy. Dave looked and saw that her body was still slouched beside him in the truck.

Surrounding the spirit Christy in a very large circular tunnel was an even brighter green light that spun a horizontal vortex. Well behind the apparition, at the end of this tunnel, was a door. It was a standard wooden door with a crystal doorknob. The door was well maintained but plain, without any ornate decorations. It reminded Dave of the doors that he saw on the professor's offices at the University of Oregon.

The door was closed, but bright white light forced its way through the doorframe and in between the hinges, covering a small part of the large green tunnel.

From that tunnel, a pathway of golden colored bricks made of light slowly crept forward. The door, the tunnel and the pathway on which the womanlike specter of Christy stood were all now suspended in black space and surrounded by ever expanding and bright shining stars. The new universe had overtaken the water beneath the lake.

Dave was stunned and taken back by the sheer grandeur and immensity of what was now before him. Christy's ethereal presence was reaching for his hand. He knew that now he was also dead.

CHAPTER 25

The truck hit the bottom of the lake, first the back, followed by the front. It bounced for a second, stirring some mud and then it settled down calmly. The impact released Dave's safety belt. The windows finally gave way and the pressure of rushing water completed filling the cab. It surrounded the two expired bodies. The shells of the deceased couple floated listlessly in their watery tomb.

Part IV
COHERENCE

*"Yeah we all shine on. Like the moon
and the stars and the sun . . ."*
—(John Lennon)

CHAPTER 26

Dave was outside of his body, transported, and was now standing near Christy's spirit on that same strange pathway of yellow brick light that came forth from the vortex. He asked her, "is this it? Is this our end?"

She responded, "there is no real end . . . only experience. Linear time is an illusion."

Dave was confused. "So, you mean its all like a record that just keeps repeating itself?"

She continued, "we have to learn, in order to move on. That is the only way to achieve real, unconditional love and acceptance . . . and to become one with the universe and the spiritual light."

Dave asked, "is this heaven?"

She replied, "heaven was created by humans as an explanation for this unknown, for this universal energy connection between everything."

"But I don't . . . I don't' understand. Are *you* Christy?"

"Charlotte, Christy, Ashley . . . it's all me in one way or another. My energy and my *soul*! I am meant to be with you . . . always. Our energy is the same piece of light." The spirit pointed beneath the glowing brick pathway and said, "look below us."

Dave looked down and could suddenly see through the golden bricks of the path. What he saw seemed like a movie playing of Canyon Lake. He was looking down on it from miles above, but he could see everything clearly.

Under the water, he could distinguish the two bodies floating, lifeless, in the cab of the truck, where it rested on the lake floor under several hundred feet of dark water.

She continued, "See the truck. See our empty shells. That is what is left of Christy and Dave, of our physical beings. That particular experience is now over for us."

"But, you mean that others, our friends and coworkers, are still going through that experience as we stand here and watch?" This was getting to be too much for Dave to comprehend.

She replied, "In a sense, yes, but at the same time, no. There is no linear time from beginning to end. It is just time."

As Dave looked back to her, her spirit steadily glided toward him. He was not afraid. She moved in front of him and they were face to face. He could see her eyes, but they seemed to go on forever. They shined lightly from her face, casting it in a hue of jade green; the same green of the tunnel, but softer and warmer. The same green of her eyes from every other life experience.

Her voice softened, "the energy is what runs through everything in the universe. Everything is connected. We have our piece, but we are still part of the whole. We incarnate into physical beings to gain knowledge and share experiences. Eventually, the experiences transform into love, the unity that defines everything as one and crosses all planes of existence."

After a few seconds, Dave spoke and said, "Well then, who am I? I guess that was you trying to reach me before? But, why did you call me Kennedy?"

"You already know. You have seen your future life . . . *our* future life together. You will be Kennedy and I will be Ashley as you have seen her. You have witnessed what you will become. That is always how it happens, you see the future just before the passing."

"Like your whole life flashing before your eyes thing? Like that?"

"Exactly. Everyone finds out, or technically *remembers* what they already knew just before they are to move on to the next experience."

Dave said, "so the flash of light, that was when I began to see the life of Kennedy? *My* future life? And then, I came back to falling in the truck? What about all of the ghost visits where, I guess, *you* were there? And how could *you* be there, if technically you were with me in the truck?"

"This is all part of the coping with moving on. Once the energy is in a body and in an experience, the mind does not want to let go and accept that there was a before and an after of some kind."

Dave asked, "how can so much happen in such a short amount of time? It seemed so real, I felt that I *was* Kennedy, but I *am* Dave. This must have happened in five minutes, or less. How can that be?"

"For the energy, time as a linear device is irrelevant. It is a construct to help people function within the context of their experience, to keep their bearings, but it is not linear once one is released and returned to the universal energy."

Dave said, "but this isn't right. I have to fix *this* life right now. I need . . . *WE* need to go back. I want another chance!"

"You must accept what is and let go of what was in order to move on."

"But, but . . . I'm not ready. What if I don't want to move on? There's so much more I need to do."

"Please. Please, take my hand."

"Why? Why can't I go back down there? We can crawl back in our bodies and swim to the surface . . ."

The spirit of Christy interrupted. "Please. You have known this all before, but by resisting, you are keeping your mind and energy from moving forward to remember it all."

Dave stared into the endless swirling green of her eyes and hesitantly took her hand because he knew that somewhere deep down, she was right. He could feel that she was right.

She moved his hand to her chest. Just as his hand reached her heart and she closed her eyes, he began to say, "What is thi . . ."

His mind flashed. He reeled through the previous lives. All of the experiences that he had ever been a part of were converging on him at that one moment.

There were numerous voices and smells and sounds all at once. He was a man in the 1930's, wearing a mechanic's outfit. He saw the dust of Oklahoma.

Then, he was a small boy playing baseball in the Bay Area. He hugged his mother after getting into a fight at school. He was a college senior graduating and receiving a diploma in Oregon. He was at his mother's funeral. He was decorating the picture of his coworker Candy in the Imaging Center. He saw his father waiving goodbye to him. He saw Christy getting out of her car without an umbrella in the Oregon rain.

It was all there, right up until the point where he drove off of the cliff and there was that bright flash of light. That was when his mind began the coping and transitional mechanism of showing him his future life as Kennedy, preparing him for the next incarnation. Though the dream of Kennedy took but seconds, his mind lived it as if it were years.

Suddenly, he was all knowing and completely understanding of what was going on and what he needed to do. It all clicked, like it had in times of incarnation before. He would now leave the shell of David and that experience willingly, as he had done many times before.

He realized that Christy's female energy had been with him in every experience; like the Yin and Yang. They were two parts of the same puzzle, looking for that perfect fit in time and space, in order to live at peace in a physical experience.

Dave saw the two of them in the white BMW driving near the ocean. He saw them sipping cabernet and cooking dinner together, with *their* cat Emily at their feet. *Yes, it makes sense now. This is what's to come.* He knew that they would rejoin. There was no more physical or emotional pain, only peace and joy and calm and understanding.

She said, "I have also gone through the same enlightening that you have. We are together now, and we'll be together next time around."

"Yes, I have seen it."

"You understand that you *must* pass . . . *We* must pass through the door . . . together."

Dave looked to the floating bodies below them in the truck and then looked up and said, "I was shown my future in terms of my current experience and because of that I could understand it properly. I remember now that the details of the future are determined *after* our energies pass through the door."

She replied, "yes, specifics aren't finalized, but our future experience is now in place. Choices affect everything. But, we are to finally be together . . . in peace and love."

He looked down at his hand and saw that he too was now only a form, an outline caught somewhere between translucent and transparent and he shared her same blue aura. He looked back to her.

She whispered, "It is time."

He replied, "Yes. I am ready."

He lightly reached up and gripped her hand. They walked up the golden pathway, side by side, hand in hand, toward the door. Together, their blue essences shined twice as brightly, but as one.

They both stood in front of the door. The white light grew stronger and pushed its way further through the spaces around the door. It was as if whatever was behind the door was anticipating their arrival, calling them home and welcoming them. Still holding hands, they both reached for the doorknob. As they touched it, the crystal turned white with light.

He had a quick, final thought, just as they grabbed the knob. It was a passage from a book that he hadn't read yet; Stephen King's, "Wolves of the Calla." It read, *"The mind prepares itself for death by offering some wonderful final hallucination, the actual semblance of an entire life."*

In those few moments before dying, he had envisioned nearly an entire life as Kennedy. *Einstein was right, time is relative.*

The two looked at each other, smiled and then faced forward again toward the door. As they turned the knob, the light from the doorknob began to show through their hands.

The door opened and they stepped through, both of them feeling the overpowering rush of serenity and oneness as it took them in.

There was a brilliantly bright flash of light. And then it was gone.

CPSIA information can be obtained
at www.ICGtesting.com
Printed in the USA
BVHW072121260521
608199BV00001B/170